D1090078

Never Trust The
One You Love

T.L. Joy

Mahogany Publications

Detroit   Ann Arbor

ISBN-13: 978-0615653853

Book cover Designed by: Kellie Dennis from Book Cover By Design
Photo from: ©iStockphoto.com/richarduphur
www.mahoganypublications.com

DEDICATION

This novel is dedicated to my loving Mother

my best friend, Tami,

and to all my friends and supporters, who were

there from day one...

I love and appreciate you all!

CONTENTS

ACKNOWLEDGMENTS

This book is more than just a novel, it will forever be a part of me. The seed of this novel was planted long ago and with the love and support of all my friends and family, I'm happy to have published my first work of art. Special thanks to my grandmother, my mother, Tami, and Tony for your love and support. I also send thanks to Charlston and Stephen for being there when I bugged you so many times about this novel. Once again, to all my family, friends, and supporters, thank you all.

Interlude:

Who would have thought that this is where I would end up? After finally having what was mine, what I deserved, shit... What I fucking earned. This is it? All the blood, the sweat, and the tears that was shed for me to end up here! Who would've thought? As I sat parked across the street from his house, I stared off into space, thinking about what I was about to do. I took a deep breath before pulling out my glock, and quietly yet quickly got out of my car. I took cautious steps as I headed towards the back of the house. With the security code imprinted in my memory, I cut off his alarm system. Sliding the glass door open, I snuck into the house and crept up the spiral staircase. I quietly entered his room where I spotted him lying there, sleeping so peacefully. Tears started to form in my eyes as I cocked the gun, and aimed it at his head. This was not any, random guy. This was my Husband, my love, my heart, and the father of my child! Just then he stirred in his sleep, and his eyes slowly began to open. The tears started to cascade down my face as I pulled the trigger............ BOOM!

<u>Introducing Smooth</u>

"Welcome to Metro Detroit" the voice of the pilot traveled through my ears as my plane landed at my new destination. Last time I was here I lost everything but this time I'm here to take what's mine... what I deserve. My father worked so hard to build his empire and it is up to me to keep our legacy going. The streets are all I know and I was determined to make the streets of Detroit my own.

As soon I made my way through the airport the first person I locked eyes with was Samya aka. Ms. Detroit. Standing at 5'6" with smooth cinnamon brown skin and long curly black hair Samya may appear to be nothing but a pretty girl but she was an upcoming force to be reckoned with. Not only was she connected with the street legends she was a cold blooded killa' struggling to make her name known as the top hit man in the city. Yet, with my help I could take her to the next level.

"Wassup Smooth?" Samya gleamed with excitement. "We got a lot to talk about." She chimed in. "Yeah, you ready to roll?" I replied, as I looked around to see all the random faces crowding around us. You never know who could be watching us so we had to move fast. Without hesitation Samya grabbed my bags and led me to her Range Rover. "Well shit, look at you... movin' up in the world." I joked as I hopped into her ride. I've known Samya for years back when her family worked for my pops. They lived in the slums and none of them made any progress ... until now.

"Shit, you know I do what I have to do. Working for the Street Legends ain't nothing to play with boy. They make that real bread." She explained. "But I know that linking you up with them will really help you get a feel for how things get down out here. This shit ain't nothin' like New York I tell ya'." She continued as we headed down the freeway. I nodded my head in agreement. One thing I learned over time was to sit back and listen. Although I had great knowledge of the streets and of the Street Legends through my father, that was something Samya would never know. You play the person to your advantage and you move on... simple as that and it was time to let Samya do her work.

First thing Samya did was introduce me to Isaac, the leader of the Street Legends. Everything about him was powerful and I knew that he would be someone I would have to keep my eye on. Isaac had reach in these streets and I knew that I had to handle him with care. Lucky for me, he knew my father and his reputation of having the best drug connect from overseas.

"You a young mothafucka' but I'll work with you kid." Isaac began, as he sat at his desk smoking his cigar. I quickly glanced at the six men surrounding him with their holsters filled with heat. Three men on one side of Isaac, and three men on the other side, all ready to kill for their boss. Secretly, I envied him. Had my father been alive, this would have been his new territory and Isaac would be six feet under. Yet, as of today I had to play my role.

"I know all about ya' pops and his work. It's a shame to hear about what happened to him son, and I know it was hard on you." "Yes sir, it was. But I got to do what I have to do to make sure our legacy lives on." I said, as I showed him my sincerity. Although I wanted to handle Isaac myself on behalf of my father I knew that Isaac had loose ends that needed to be tied. So what better way to get my revenge than by letting his loose ends take care of him as I sit back and watch.

Isaac and I quickly adjourned our meeting with an agreement of me exchanging my Colombian imports for a piece of the territory my father had previously agreed to take over before his death. Although it was not the whole territory that was supposed to be given to him it was a start. In order to survive out here I had to keep my enemies close and create a name for myself. I was only sixteen at the time, getting ready to embark on something big in my new hometown. All I needed was a team.

Samya continued to show me around and introduce me to important people that I needed to know. Yet no one was more important than the dynamic duo Kris and his girl Krazy. "Word on the street is that Kris is good at making hits and his girl is good at setting niggas up. Those two together is crazy I tell ya'! " Samya chimed in, as we drove over to their spot on the east side of Detroit.

"And no one claimed them yet?" I asked out of curiosity. "Naw, I don't know why, but hey, with me and them on your team you will be good to go." Samya answered with full support. I loved her support yet I knew Samya was not on the level of Kris as far as hits. Samya was messy and not good at calculating. While Kris was cold, calculated, and could do his hits without a trace. All of his murders were left unsolved while Samya left evidence and wanted to be known for her work. I couldn't have someone like that be on my team for long which is why I had Samya bring me to her replacements.

Standing on the corner dressed in nothing but a wife beater, some Levi's, and some black and white Jordan's on this hot summer day was the infamous Kris. His fuzzy braids, to the slashes in his eyes brows, and the tats on his arms showed that he didn't give a fuck and had nothing to lose. That was the type of person I wanted on my team. Not some flashy nigga living beyond his means. In due time he would get flashy as the money would come in, but not while he was starting from the bottom.

"So you the nigga that wants to meet me huh? I heard from ya' girl Samya that you were coming here to make a takeover. But what you want from me?" was the first thing that came out of Kris's mouth when he first laid eyes on me. "I want you to be on my team to help me take what's mine... shit, and get what's

4

yours. I know you tired of these lil niggas apart of the AK47 and the Street Legends running shit out here living the good life, while you working hard for yours and still struggling. But if you join my team, we can come together and make shit happen." I suggested, playing upon his emotions. I could see in his eyes that he was tired of living like this and as long as I showed him that I can make a way out of no way, he would join me without hesitation.

Kris stood there thinking long and hard about the next move he was going to make. "Aiight, I hear you... but what is the name of this shit if I'm going to be a part of it?" He asked. "The Hot Boyz." I answered. His face lit up and his eyes gleamed with joy. "Hell yeah I'm with that shit, let's take these lil' niggas down and get what's ours. But if shit doesn't pan out the way you said it would I'll kill you myself. And that's a promise nigga." Kris warned me, but little does he know that I had this shit mapped before I even got here. There was no doubt that shit would go as planned. Now all I needed was a down ass bitch to take care of home.

Introducing Sweetz:

Nothin' in my life has ever been perfect. I lived with a mother who had a fucked up mental. When she loved, she loved hard. No one came before her man, not even her own child. The day my mom's new boyfriend Reggie moved in was the day my life turned upside down.

Reggie was no good. Of course he treated my mom good providing her with money, conversation, and good sex. But he was a scandalous, triflin' ass, pedophile that molested me from the time I was eight, to the time I was fourteen years old. Did my mother ever know? Hell yeah she knew...but she never did anything about it since she never believed me. As always, her man came first. I couldn't take that shit. I had to get out.

At fourteen, I finally gathered the courage to pack up my shit and run away. The same night I ran away was the same night Reggie and my mother were mysteriously murdered. I guess you can say I was lucky but I don't believe in all that. Try being lucky in a fuckin' shelter with thirty dyke ass girls trying to rape you every night! I got out of one bad situation and ended up into another. That was all until I met HIM.

Smooth was his name. While I was fourteen living at the shelter he was eighteen years old running the streets of Detroit. Everyone knew about him when they heard his name. "Smooth didn't play" or "Smooth is the fuckin' man." He was the trending topic of year. His name roamed all over Michigan. If you didn't know about him, you would eventually find out. Nothing could compare to the day when I saw him standing on the corner of my street after a rough ass day at school.

"What's your name?" He asked me. "La'nay." I shyly replied. He stood there and gazed deeply in my eyes. "Where you from?" He continued. "The shelter." I answered, as I looked down at the ground. "You don't have any family or nothing around here?" "No. I don't have anybody." I said softly. I looked up at him, only to see his penetrating eyes still stuck on me. "Well you have me Sweetz." He smiled. I laughed at the nickname he gave me.

"Sweetz huh?" "Yes...Because you're the sweetest girl I ever met." He said, causing me to smile for the very first time. "Now go pack up your stuff and come with me. I will show you what a real family is all about." He commanded.

With no questions asked, I did just as he said. As a result, he followed through on his part by taking me in and showing me what family was all about. My life changed when I met Smooth. He introduced me to a whole new lifestyle of the faster and finer things. He provided me with everything I wanted and more. I had my own house in the suburbs with those from the upper class, a luxury car to get around in, and the love and support from him and his family.

Although he was my "boyfriend", Smooth was my provider, and also the leader of the new notorious gang called The Hot Boyz. I was never involved in his street life, nor did I want to be.

I continued being that fly ass bitch up in high school with my girls Krazy and Samya. We all had ties to this game so we had no choice but to be close. Other bitches couldn't understand the lifestyle we lived and the envy to be in our shoes caused us to be the most hated females in the city. Yet, no one understood that with the perks came unspoken downsides that we would be faced with and over time I quickly learned.

"Business has to be made, and someone has to do it," was the last thing Smooth said to me before he left me to go to Atlanta. By that time, I was fifteen and madly in love with Smooth. Him leaving was like someone tearing my heart out of my chest. "Baby, don't leave me." I pleaded. "Don't worry baby. I will be back. You just hold it down for me mami while I'm gone, and I will be back for you. I promise." He said smoothly, before he kissed me softly on the lips. I watched as he hopped into his car and left leaving me with a broken heart.

I thought he would be back within a couple of months, but a couple of months turned into a year, and a year have now turned into four years of Smooth being gone. During this time, Krazy and I had to do what we had to do, in order to keep up our lavish lifestyle. The streets still had to be ran even if the Hot Boyz was gone, and who else was going to do that except the lovely ladies of the affiliation. Krazy and Smooth's younger sister, Liyah, were making moves on behalf of the Hot Boyz. They were responsible for the gritty shit, while Samya and I were appointed as the "pretty faces" to lure the targeted niggas into the setup. We were a dynamic team, making shit happen for the Hot Boyz, and *bringing in the cash during the cold Detroit winter. Yet, everything changed when Samya started to act brand new.*

"I'm tired of doing this shit." She complained, as we sat in our designated car parked in front of a cheap ass motel. We were in the process of doing a job, waiting for two niggas to meet up with us. "I'm supposed to be a fuckin' hit man, doing what the fuck I do best. Not wasting my damn time being someone's decoy. All in the name of the Hot Boyz! Psssh! I got a family to feed and splitting this money four ways ain't cuttin' it." Samya continued to rant.

I held my tongue because if I said what I really wanted to say it would get ugly and tonight's job had big money potential. There was no way we could fuck this up. So instead, I stayed neutral and nonchalantly said, "Girl, just do you. Let's just finish this, and after tonight you do what you gotta' do." "I sure will, and after this I'm doing my own shit. Fuck a Hot Boyz!" Samya exclaimed, but I knew that was a bad move on her part. After that night, the woman who once pieced together the Hot Boyz was now the enemy. Although she easily walked away this time, we all knew that it was never easy to walk out of this lifestyle.

*   *   *

The summer of 2008 has finally arrived, and here I' am getting ready to spend my Friday night handling business for the Hot Boyz. Usually my girls and I spent our weekends shopping, and going to elite lounge parties. But with the Hot Boyz still in

Atlanta, Krazy and I had to make sure shit was running smoothly. We had a few errands to run before we could even go to the "Spot", which was one of the Hot Boyz private lounges to chill, and unwind on one floor but handle business on another. This was only exclusive to the Hot Boyz and some close associates that they invited. In preparation for tonight I slipped into a fitted black skirt, a red blouse that complimented my brown skin tone, and my black Christian Louboutin six inch pumps.

Time was quickly slipping away, as I rushed to style my wavy, jet black hair that stopped at my mid-back. While I added my finishing touches to my makeup, I studied myself in the mirror. My high cheekbones and exotic eyes gave me a Mediterranean look, and at nineteen years old, I was killin' this shit. Who knew that handling business could look this damn good!

All I could do was laugh to myself thinking about my past. Back when I lived in the shelter I was nowhere near the finest "Dime" of them all. I didn't have money to get my hair done, my nails done, and buy the flyest clothes. The young boys out here only wanted a flashy bitch with a fat ass. Guys would never approach me. They could care less to get to know a plain girl like me. Yet it's funny how things drastically changed after Smooth came into my life, and helped me step my image up. With the pretty face, the pearly whites, and a body to kill, I have men from here to Kingdom Come, wishing that they had a chance with me. But as I said before, "wishing" they had a chance.

Once I got done, I called Krazy up. "Hello, you speaking to the queen of the craziest." She answered jokingly, "Girl please, you know you are not a queen." I snapped while laughing. "Just like you're not sweet." she responded, causing me to suck my teeth. "Whateva', look I'm ready so where are you right now?" I asked, while cutting the lights off in the house. "Girl, I'm in your driveway right now." She said giggling. "Oh foreal! I'll be out in a minute then." I exclaimed before we both hung up.

Quickly, I grabbed my jacket, locked up the house, and went outside. There sitting in her car blasting that old school "Knuck if you buck" by Crime Mob, was the one and only Krazy. Her pretty chocolate brown skin glowed under the illuminating street lights, while her long, layered, black and red wine streaked hair, blew along with the cool Detroit wind. She studied me with her almond shaped, green eyes and flashed me her almighty Colgate smile.

One look at her and you'd think she was sweet and innocent. Many people thought we were related because we both had smooth chocolate brown skin, and an angelic face. But there was a huge difference between us. I was the sweet and calm one, never the one to start mess while she was the aggressive one, who would cuss you out or fight you in a hot second. Even with our differences, she was still my girl for life! I hopped into her black, 2008 Mercedes Benz SL class, greeting her with a joking "Hey heffa."

"Wassup trick, you ready to roll out?" She asked, while putting in her Lil Wayne Cd. "Hell yeah." I said, getting hyped up from the music. "Good, cause we already late." She added, before she started up the car and sped off.

We rapped along to the songs until she busted out laughing. "What?" I asked innocently, "Gurl, we know you are not about that life, dressing like that." She said, looking at me up and down. "Hey no one said you can't look good while handling business" I shrugged. " Shit, you can't eveeen, talk about me, while you're over there looking like that." I continued, pointing at her clothes. "Girl please! I look like I'm ready for whateva'." Krazy said full of excitement. I rolled my eyes in disgust. "Ugh, whatever. More like you got nothing to lose." I ended, while studying her attire.

A black beater and some black dickies pants was what she was dressed in, as well as the black and white Jordan 23's on her feet. "Bitch I'm about that life!" Krazy playfully joked. That was the one thing I liked about our friendship, it was authentic. Even though we had big shoes to fill and were getting a real taste of the street life that our boyfriends indulged in, we were still young girls that cherished the bond that we had.

"What will be the first thing you do when you see Smooth?" Krazy asked me. "I'mma slap the shit outta him for leaving me for four years." I quickly answered. "Girl bye, you know you are going to hop on that dick and work on a baby." Krazy busted out, causing us to both laugh. Yet all the laughter subsided as we pulled up in front of a beat up yellow house. I leaned forward puzzled at the sight. I stared at the house across the street that had shingles falling off the roof and bars across the windows, this house wasn't one of our trap houses so the reason behind us being here was unclear. I leaned back and looked at Krazy when I felt this scary aura surrounding her. The black coldness of her eyes was menacing, the slight killer smirk on her face seemed unreal.

Without a word Krazy pulled out the leather gloves out the center console and popped the trunk open. Within seconds, she sashayed across the street like an alley cat and walked up to the house with a gas can. She feverishly poured the gasoline all over the house. I sat in awe at how her moves were so calculated. She made a trail of gasoline to the resident's car, which was parked on the side of their house. I leaned closer to the window and noticed the old car had a huge puddle of oil underneath it. My mind was blown away at how Krazy could put a master plan together at a drop of the dime.

She casually walked back to the trunk and grabbed a water bottle filled with a black substance and walked back up to the car. She slide under the car and started to pour the black substance in an angle so it could run down the driveway. After Krazy got out from underneath the car she walked to the edge of the sidewalk, pulled out a cigarette and lit it with a match. She calmly inhaled the smoke into her lungs, dropped the match, and watched as the fire travel up the driveway to the car. BOOM! The loud noise filled the air as the car went up in flames catching the house on fire.

The screams and cries of people in the house rung into my ears. I saw people trying to escape the burning flames but it was too late because the house was engulfed in flames quicker than anyone could imagine. The smell of burning flesh and wood filled my nostrils. I glanced at Krazy who once had a menacing smirk, now standing close to our car, smoking her cigarette with a look of satisfaction, as the reflection of the fire danced in her cold dark eyes. I was in pure and utter shock. Never have I witnessed anything like this, let alone this side of Krazy. When she hopped back in the car I was speechless and we rode to The Spot in silence.

<u>Introducing Krazy:</u>

We pulled up to "The Spot" which was the Hot Boyz industrial building that was used to chill and store our work. This place has been the foundation to distribute our products to our lieutenants. As Sweetz and I walked into the building we were greeted by other members of the Hot Boyz team. Most of them sat at the bar chilling and sipping on their drinks, while the others threw dollars at the strippers performing on stage. We continued to walk to the back of the building to the office. Sweetz typed in the pass code to the office and as we entered we were greeted by the infamous duo Smooth and Kris.

Smooth sat behind the desk with his feet propped up smoking on a cigar as Kris stood posted against the wall sipping on his half a pint of Hennessy straight from the bottle. Pain and anger filled my body as I stared at how both of them seem so unfazed by the fact that they have been gone for four years with no contact. How could they be in our presence without one trace of remorse of what they did to Sweetz and I. My thoughts continued to flow as Smooth finally acknowledge our presence.

"So nice of you ladies to join us. I'm happy to see that our profit has doubled each year." Smooth began. "Yeah, we found a lot of flaws in your methods so we decided to implement a few new things" Sweetz replied, with attitude.

"I see and by the records it shows ya'll ideas got us top notch out here in the streets...Good job" Kris joined in. "Yeah you better give us our props after we busted our asses for the Hot Boyz." Sweetz snapped, yet Smooth and Kris laughed in response. "What the fuck is so funny?" I asked in irritation. "Aww, don't be like that Krazy you know we missed y'all. Let's stop with this small talk and give each other some love." Kris replied.

Automatically, Kris walked over to Sweetz and oddly, he hugged Sweetz for a long time while planting a gentle kiss on her cheek and pulled away smiling. Of course to any on the team this would be a sign of respect to the Boss lady but I was always kind of suspicious about Sweetz and Kris. I mean, even though I know that she's my girl for life, and wouldn't do that type of foul shit to me...It was always in the back of my mind that something wasn't right between those two. Hell, I even think her boyfriend Smooth knows what's up, but come on now, Sweetz isn't like that or is she? I just couldn't shake the emotions that were building up inside of me. My words began to spew out my mouth like vomit without any thought behind them.

"So you guys been gone for four years and you have the nerve to sit in this office like y'all runnin' shit?" I started. " Krazy hold on a min..." Sweetz started but I abruptly cut her off. "Naw fuck that, we been out here doin' numbers in these streets and ya'll wanna pop up like shit is cool? Sitting up here trying to hold a normal conversation without even a thought of explaining yourself." I ranted. " Krazy ," Smooth started calmly. "I know there is some things that we need to talk about, but for now let's enjoy this happy reunion." He smiled. " Ain't shit happy about this reunion!" I spat, causing silence to creep over the room.

I could feel the hot tears swelling up in my eyes. Everything I have been through since they were gone quickly disappeared. I glared at Kris with every ounce of hate I had in my body. Kris stood about 6'1" with that smooth chocolate brown complexion, and a set of deep and mysterious gray eyes that pierced into my soul. His single, black braids flowed to his shoulders, and the three slashes in his eyebrows, and the tattoo that said "Hot Boyz 4 Life" on his arm gave him a tough and edgy look. Yet the Killa K tattoo on his wrist lets me know that he is still has a soft spot for me. Even though I was mad at Kris, I still loved his sexy ass.

"I think you and Kris have a lot to talk about. Same for me and Sweetz. So we are going to give you guys some privacy" Smooth suggested, breaking my thoughts. "Yeah, you do that" I replied, as Sweetz and Smooth made their exit, leaving Kris and I alone.

"You staring at me like you want to put me six feet under." Kris said, staring back at me. "Shit, maybe I do." I snapped back. "Why you gotta be so angry Krazy?" Kris asked. "Four years of holding shit down. Building this shit back up while you're in Atlanta doing God knows what, and I'm supposed to be happy go lucky? Really Kris, what do you expect from me?" I yelled with anger. " What the fuck do you expect from this game? Shit happens, moves had to be made and if you riding with me you gotta' be a down ass bitch." Kris yelled. "Nobody wanted to be a part of this shit Krazy, but we gotta' eat and we gotta' survive. If you can't handle this shit then I suggest you get the fuck outta' Michigan and find yo' way." He concluded, causing my eyebrow to quickly raise from his response.

"Oh really? Is that how you feel? Nigga you need me just as much as I need you. Don't play that shit with me." I began. "That's some straight up bullshit and I should beat the shit out of you for even saying some fucked up shit like that." I was so mad, that tears of anger began to flow down my cheek. But that didn't stop me! I just kept cussing and going off, while Kris stood there staring blankly at me. Before I could finish cussing him out, Kris grabbed me, and planted a kiss full of hot, fiery passion onto my lips. I felt myself getting into this kiss, but the thought of what he just said caused me to push him away.

"Fuck you Kris! Don't try to kiss on me like it's ok... You're nothing but a..." I started but Kris quickly cut me off. " Krazy, do you really think I'm about to leave yo' ass like that? I love you too much to do that shit to you, but you gotta realize that in this game it ain't always sunshine and roses. We don't live like the others. I need you to hold me down like I hold you down. And trust me baby, when we get this money and can no longer be a part of this shit.....Shit, I'll wife you up and put a ring on it. Do things the right way, but you gotta be patient aiight?"

Kris just said everything that deep down inside I've been waiting to hear from him. All I could do was nod and smile in response. I loved that man with all my being. There was nothing else to say, all I could do was kiss him once again. He pulled me closer to him by my waist, as our tongues explored each other's mouth. I let out a slight moan before I broke the kiss. I pushed Kris back onto the desk and straddled his lap.

We began to deeply tongue kiss, while we slowly grinded on each other. His hands roamed over every curve of my body, while he gently sucked on the left side of my neck. I began to moan loudly because it was one of my hot spots, and he pleased me just right. While Kris pulled off my beater and unhooked my red bra, I pulled off his shirt, revealing his sexy eight pack, and tribal tattoo on his chest. Once all clothes hit the floor, we were going at it, right in the Smooth's office. Not giving a damn if anyone walked in on us.

<u>Sweetz:</u>

I couldn't believe that standing before my eyes was the infamous Smooth.   One look at him, and I could've melted right there. Any girl with a set of eyes would have wet their panties just by looking at him. Smooth was a one in a million that women often dreamed about. Even those who despised caramel men with a passion would change their mind quickly when they laid eyes on him.

Standing at a strong 6'3" with a medium built body that girls craved , Smooth had a God given sexiness. His smooth caramel skin was accented by those rare and mesmerizing honey brown colored eyes. His wavy black hair was always in the freshest crossover braids that stopped at his mid-back. His "I'm a Boss" swag gave him an extra sex appeal. Not one man in town could touch what Smooth had, and I was proud to say he was all mine!

"Damn I missed you Sweetz." He greeted in his sexy smooth voice. "Four fuckin years, you better have missed my ass." I tried to stay mad at him but it was so hard. He placed his hand over his heart and acted like he was offended. "Aww, so that's all I get? I don't get no hug, no love, no nothin'!" He started, while giving me his sad puppy dog eyes. "Girl, you haven't seen me in four years, and you act like you don't even want me anymore. You betta' give ya' man a hug and show me some love." He smiled.

I laughed before I decided to stop fronting on him. This is Smooth we're talking about here. My one and only love! To his surprise, I squealed while jumping on him. All eyes were on us in the lounge, but I didn't give a damn. "I missed you so much baby." I continued, hugging him tightly. "Me too baby, me too." He laughed, revealing those adorable, deep dimples that pierced into his cheek. I slid off him and stared up at his sexy frame.

We quickly made our way to a vacant booth and ordered our drinks while T-pain played throughout the spot. Sitting back in a relaxed manner, Smooth eyed me up and down. "Damn I know you hate my ass right now." He sighed full of guilt. "But I never wanted to leave you ma'...It wasn't my choice to go. Believe me." "I know that it wasn't your choice Smooth." I answered in a light voice. "But, I'm back now baby girl." Smooth smiled, while embracing me tightly.

That was the thing that I loved about Smooth. He could always make me feel so happy, even when I was so down and out. Especially with the sex! I mean, even though he's a well-respected Boss, he knew how to respect women and treat them like a queen. Unlike Kris! Even though Kris is Krazy's man, we all knew that Kris is known for cheating, as well as beating on women. I would know! He might not do it to Krazy, but we all know how some of these street niggas are. Luckily, I found a good one.

"I can't believe you were out there handling business while I was gone." Smooth said, instantly reminding me of the horrific shit that I witnessed. "Can't believe I did too." I said before taking another sip. "I know you probably witnessed some shit that you never been exposed to before, but this life ain't always what you think it is. It ain't easy being a part of the Hot Boyz." Smooth explained. "But trust me baby, this is the first and last time I will expose you to some shit like that." Smooth finished, as he stared deeply into my eyes. From that moment I knew he wasn't telling me no lies, and after what I witnessed with Krazy I was glad of it.

"Speaking of the Hot Boyz, where's Killa' Mike? I haven't seen him in a while." I quickly changed the subject to something lighter. Smooth chuckled. "That's right, you haven't. He's somewhere around here." "Well, I'm not gonna' go look for him. Cause shiit, I'm too tired." I responded, leaning back onto the seat.

"Should've known, with your little lazy ass." A deep male voice from behind me snapped quickly. Ready to curse whoever it was out, I turned around, and spotted the one and only Killa' Mike.

Standing at 5'9', at 17-years-old, Killa' Mike had a smooth butterscotch complexion. His wavy black hair, from his black and Puerto Rican bloodline, was braided in crisscross braids under a Detroit fitted cap. One look at him and you'd say "Aww." He was overall loveable, funny, and just hard to resist. His sexy light brown eyes, deep left dimple, and soft pink lips matched perfectly with his frame. He was more than cute, he was damn near sexy like Smooth.

The Lil' Killa Mike was looking too good on this night. Sporting a clean Gucci white tee under a black leather bomber jacket, some crisp blue jeans and brand new Jordan's too match. If only he wasn't Smooth's little brother, because the things I could've done to that boy would have been off the charts!

"Mikeyyyy!" I exclaimed, as I got up and gave him a hug. "Wassup mami." He smiled, while taking my hand and getting a good look at me. "Got-damn girl! You look too good, if you weren't with my brother, just imagine all the things I'd do to you." He licked his lips. "Watch it Lil' homie, before you say something to get ya' ass beat." Smooth snapped. I could tell he was getting heated. "Dayum playa', calm down! I was only playing with her." Mike said, throwing his hands up in the air. "You betta' just be playin' with her. Or I'll fuck ya' ass up." Smooth replied, taking a gulp of his drink. I sucked my teeth in the midst of it all. "Boy, stop acting like that to Mikey." I said, pinching Mike's soft cheeks. "But baby..." Smooth pleaded. "But baby nothin'!" I said ending him. "Ooo...She got you in check homie." Mike laughed until Smooth shot him the coldest look.

"So anyways, how you doin' mami?" Mike asked, quickly changing the subject. "I'm doin good, you?" I responded. "Shit, I'm doin' good! All these ladies are looking fine as hell up in here. I might have to take one of these shorties home with me tonight, and show them how I do it." Mike said, wandering off the topic.

"Boy please, you wish you had something to show them." I said sarcastically. "Forreal." Smooth agreed with me, while laughing. "Whateva', I got the six pack and other things to work with." He smiled, showing off his nicely toned abs. "Boy please, you mean a two-pack." I cracked on him, knowing that he was right. "Man, ya'll some haters." He stated, blowing us off.

At that moment, a super thick, big booty, brown skinned girl walked past. Giving him a welcoming smile and eye wink. "Well, that's my cue! I'm out." He said, smiling righteously. "Bye." Smooth and I added in unison. "Peace!" Mike joked in a deep, playful voice.

Running after the girl, he yelled out to get her attention, once again. "Aye girl! Yeah you, I see ya' baby! Aww...Don't act like you don't see me... Aww, so you wanna run away from me huh? Well I'm right behind you mami!"

Smooth and I laughed loudly at what just happened. "That boy is too crazy." I said smiling. "Yep, that's Mike for ya'." Smooth agreed with a smirk. "I know that's right." I added. I was happy that things were going to be back to normal. I could play my role as the boss lady, and the whole crew would be back up here running shit. Yet, I was even more excited to go home with Smooth and show him just how much I missed his sexy ass. The look in Smooth's eye let me know that he couldn't wait either.

"Let's go get head to my crib so we can catch up on old times." Smooth suggested, while licking his lips, and rubbing his hands together. I smiled in response as I quickly got up and made my way to the exit, with Smooth traveling behind me. We made our way to the parking lot, and quickly hopped into his Escalade. Smooth was known to never conform with the masses, which was why his car was candy painted cobalt blue, with black flames accented on the sides.

Lil Wayne's "A Milli" Blasted loudly in the car, while we were on our way to the Hot Boyz mansion. During the ride, we talked about whatever popped in our mind, while he rubbed in-between my thighs, and I massaged his hardness below in my hands. This was a normal routine for our car rides only because we're just freaks like that. It took only an hour before we pulled up in front of his huge mansion. The property was lit up by the lights of the two water fountains in his huge yard, making me feel like royalty.

"Gotta' love the good life huh?" I said, admiring the landscape. "Yeah, well you know how I do ma' " Smooth smiled, while popping his collar. "Any-who." I said harshly, after rolling my eyes and sucking my teeth. "Oooh, ok I see how you are. I see how you treat me." Smooth joked. "Boy please, so are we gonna' go in or what?" I asked playfully with an attitude. "Well c'mon then." He replied, taking my hand and leading me to the front door. Smooth rung the doorbell, and automatically a deep voice began to speak. "Who is it? " "It's Smooth, so open up the door!" Smooth yelled back.

Just then, the door opened revealing Pistol. Another Hot Boy who was quick to fight, but also quick to shoot. That's why they called him Pistol. I have to admit, Pistol is scary. Yet he can be nice... only when he wants to be. He stood about 6'5" with light skin and large, round, cold black eyes.

His muscular arms were covered with thousands of tattoos, many consisting of the names and faces of those close to him that died. His hair was in a bald fade cut but was always covered with hats. His soft and pouty lips was just too tempting to kiss, and gave him a huge resemblance to L.L Cool J' with his sexy ass.

"Oh my bad Smooth, I thought you were some bad ass kids playin' pranks." Pistol apologized while letting us in. I could instantly feel his eyes roaming my body, but I shook it off. "Naw, never that." Smooth simply remarked, giving Pistol some dap. "You remember my girl Sweetz right?" Smooth asked, placing his hands around my waist tightly. "Yeah, wassup mami?" Pistol greeted with a smirk.

"Nothin much." I hugged him friendly. "Wassup with you?" I asked, pulling away with a sweet smile. "The hell if I know ma' " Pistol answered, walking into the living room. Smooth and I followed him, step by step while holding hands. As soon as I stepped in the living room, I was knocked out by the intoxicating scent of Purple Haze. "Look, I gotta go to the bathroom, so I'll be back ok?" Smooth ensured us. "Ok." We added in unison.

I watched as Smooth trailed down the hall. Pistol started smoking once again while staring at me with those underestimated eyes. He exhaled the smoke with his mouth and nose before he spoke. "Sweetz, Sweetz, Sweetz...Still that pretty ass Sweetz."

I giggled in response. "You still that quick tempered Pistol."
"You got that shit right." Pistol laughed, taking another puff of his purple haze. "So ma, you still friends with Krazy and Samya?" He asked. I nodded in response. "Good, good. So you know that Johntae died right?" Pistol said, bringing up a former member of the Hot Boyz crew. "Yeah, it's a shame isn't it?" I replied, shaking my head.

Without me sensing it, Smooth came behind me wrapping his arms around my waist. "What's a shame ma'?" He asked being nosey. "Nothin." I quickly said. "Oh, ok...Well Pistol we're going upstairs aiight?" Smooth suggested. "Aiight see ya' Sweetz." Pistol said, winking his eye at me. "Yeah, I'll see ya' " I smiled, and followed Smooth upstairs to his room. I stood there admiring how fly his room was, not even paying attention to him behind me.

"You ready for me to put you to sleep?" Smooth asked in a sexy voice, sending chills up my spine. I closed my eyes as he began licking, and sucking on one of my hot spots on my neck causing me to moan. "Mmm...you know it papi." I moaned. "Good, now get out of those clothes." He commanded as he pulled away and smacked me roughly on my ass. With no hesitation, I went into the bathroom and changed into a silk red, teddy set that I left the last time I paid a visit.

Usher's "Seduction" played loudly while I went back into the bedroom only to see Smooth sitting on the bed with nothing on but his boxers...Damn, he looks good. I stood in the doorway, staring at his chest glistening under the dimmed light. He looked up at me with those honey colored eyes, and licked his luscious lips. Those lips that made me melt. Smooth patted his leg as a cue to tell me to come and sit on daddy's lap. I bit down on my bottom lip as I walked over to him sexy, but slowly switching my hips.

Once I made my way up to him, I straddled myself onto his lap, and slowly started to deeply tongue kiss him as he squeezed my ass. Our tongues explored each other's mouths as he pulled off my top revealing the erect nipples of my breasts. One look at them and it was over. He placed my right nipple into his willing lips and began to suck, nip, and lick at it while he pinched and massaged my left nipple.

I moaned from the pleasure he was giving me and began to suck his spot on his neck. Smooth groaned from pleasure, causing my pussy to get even wetter. I glided my tongue over his snake tattoo and bit down on it, causing him to whimper in mild pain. Yet I continued to suck on that same spot, making it feel numb and pleasurable. He laid back on the bed and rolled over so that he was on top of me. Starving to feel him inside me, I aggressively pulled down his boxers, revealing the nice, long, and thick twelve inches that was calling my name. I couldn't keep my mouth off it. I sucked his dick until he begged me to stop. I pulled away, as I licked my lips and grabbed the handcuffs from the dresser next to the bed. Before we knew it, Smooth was cuffed up to the bed while I rode his dick like a crazy jockey. While in reverse cowgirl, I bounced my ass up and down, giving him a beautiful scenery as I creamed all over his dick. I rode that dick so good, he couldn't keep his mouth closed!

Finally, Smooth was uncuffed and in control. I wrapped my legs around his waist tightly, while I bit down on his wide shoulders and dug my acrylic nails into his bare back. "Mmm, keep goin' baby." I moaned and whimpered into his ear. "Uhhhh...You ain't said nothing but a word." Smooth groaned in pleasure. Just then, Smooth pulled his dick all the way out and pushed it all back in, quickly hitting my g-spot. I screamed loudly, so that the whole neighborhood could hear me screaming.

He continued hitting that exact spot harder and faster, blowing me out of my mind. This went on for hours with me cumin on countless times. I squirted out my love, as he came inside me during our final climax. We collapsed onto the bed, trying to catch our breath, as we both were dripping in sweat. I laid my head on his chest, while he held me tightly, and played with my hair as I slowly started to fall asleep. For the first time in four lonely years, I felt what has been a stranger to me...safe and loved. But now that I'm back in his arms, I felt it all come back to me, feeling just like I did when I was fifteen years old.

The next morning I woke up wrapped tightly in the arms of Smooth. Just the thought of last night had me smiling like the Kool-Aid man! I finally got my man back and everything is coming back to the way it was. Sooner or later, things will be perfect...Right?

I continued lying in the bed, staring at the wall in deep thought until my cell phone rung. I tried to free myself from Smooth, but he wouldn't let go, and would only pull me closer to him. Doing the best I could, I reached over, and grabbed my phone off the nightstand.

"Hello." I whispered. "Sweetz..." The voice of Samya traveled through my phone. "What's wrong?" I asked with full concern. " Turn on the news..." Was all she said. Without hesitation I grabbed the remote and turned to the channel 7 news, only to see a report on the same house that I witnessed being set on fire. "They're all dead... My whole family. My brother and I are the only ones alive only 'cause we went to run some errands." She cried, as my heart sunk in my chest. " I don't know what to do... I-I Don't know who would do this to me..." She rambled in confusion. "But I do know that I have to get out the Hot Boyz for good. Tell Smooth that I'll see him today for the meeting." Samya said before abruptly hanging up.

I laid back down in confusion to why Krazy would do such a horrible thing to Samya. I mean, I know Samya fucked up by trying to leave the Hot Boyz, but killing her whole family though? It ain't that deep... or is it? "Who was that ?" Smooth asked, quickly interrupting my thoughts. His eyes were still closed, but he looked too sexy. "That was Samya..." I paused.

"What did she want ?" He pondered. "That was her family on the news. Someone lit their house on fire and they died." I explained. "What the fuck?" Smooth jumped up. "Is someone trying to prove a point to the Hot Boyz? Fuck that, we gotta' find this shit out today!" Smooth's temper began to flare, yet I rushed to calm him down. "Not quite babe. Samya left the Hot Boyz a while ago. She told me to tell you she will be at the meeting to leave the Hot Boyz for good."

" For good huh? Yeah aiight, that little bitch will be back before you know it. Begging to have another shot with the Hot Boyz just watch." Smooth laughed. Yet, deep down inside I knew that with Krazy being behind Samya's loss, all hell was going to break loose. It's just a matter of time.

I slipped out the bed, covered my naked body with my robe, and stomped down the long hallway to the bedroom of Kris and Krazy. As I made my way to their bedroom, I could hear the screams of Samya's family ringing in my ear. I stormed into their room and screamed at the top of my lungs "You killed them! I can't believe that you killed them!"

Kris was the first one to wake up and respond. "What the fuck are you talking about?" "Krazy! You killed Samya's family." I revealed, as serious as this was I felt as if there were no reason to hold any punches. I wanted to get a clear understanding today.

Krazy opened her eyes and chuckled. "That's what that bitch gets!" "Wha- Why?" was all I could say in pure confusion. Krazy's cheerful expression quickly turned into anger and irritation as she threw her cover off and sat up in the bed." I said that's what that bitch get! Bitches always think they slick trying to sneak in and take yo' fam from ya' and shit. So I took hers before it could even go down! Fuck her, Fuck her family and fuck anyone who feels sorry for the worthless bitch!"

Before anyone could say a word, Krazy hopped out of her bed and stormed into the bathroom. The sound of the shower running and Lil Boosie "Betrayed" blasting from the speakers began to fill the room. I stood there in astonishment. How could she act as if killing a former friend's family was justified? Although Krazy and I have been friends for a long time, I could not comprehend this. I know Samya may have fucked up here and there, but what family did she take from Krazy?

Kris and I looked to each other for a moment before he shrugged his shoulders, rolled comfortably back over into his bed, and quickly fell asleep. All I could do is shake my head. Kris was a typical street nigga, that would just to roll the fuck over and go to sleep while his chick is obviously upset. He didn't even blink an eye when I told him that Krazy killed Samya's family.

Once again my days of keeping my head in the sand were over. Smooth kept me so sheltered and away from his street life that I never knew just how ugly this game really was. Better yet how fucked up the people involved were. Disgusted from what I witnessed, I made my exit from their room, and headed downstairs for a much needed cup of tea to clear my mind.

Krazy

I stood under the shower head and allowed the water to run down my body. No one could understand how much pain I felt right now. Samya and any other bitch deserved to lose their life or their family's life, if they ever think of taking my family away from me.

I can still remember like it happened yesterday when Sweetz and I stopped by one of the Hot Boyz's mansions to make sure the cleaning staff got paid. The head housekeeper Maria pulled me to the side and handed me a Ziploc bag filled with a pair of orange lace panties that was too small to be mine! Maria filled me in on eye opening info before she bowed her head and exited the room. It was funny how everyone thought I had no clue about Kris and his cheating ways, but I always kept tabs on him by paying the head housekeepers at all of the mansions to keep me updated on Kris and his hoes. Yet that day I discovered that the most recent hoe was Samya's trickin' ass!

Rage instantly filled my body and I couldn't control myself. I had to take away her family just so she can experience exactly how I felt, every time someone decided to lay down with my man. Every bitch that Kris fucks gets put six feet under. Kris was not just the love of my life, but the only family I had. For that reason, I couldn't let any bitch step on my toes.

So many thoughts ran through my mind as I stepped out the shower and wrapped my red robe around my body. Sweetz was so naive when it came to the street life. Although these past four years has shown her some things or two, there was so much that she would never be able to grasp. I loved Sweetz like a sister but I knew that we were two different types of girls. Sweetz was made to be the bosses' lady, to stay fly and play house while I was the ride or die bitch, that was a natural born killer and too cutthroat to play house. Even though there were plenty days that I wished I could live a normal life and become a wife to Kris...Hopefully if we play our cards right that would happen.

I walked back into the bedroom, only to see Kris fast asleep. I stood there and stared at him with nothing less than love and admiration. We had a few hours to relax before our Hot Boyz meeting, so I laid next to my man, taking in his powerful aura. The love that I have for Kris is so deep that I promise I will kill anyone who thinks or decides to come between that!

<u>Samya</u>

5 O'clock was the time of reckoning with the Hot Boyz. Today will be my final meeting before I work solo on my own shit. I pulled up to the spot wearing my all black sweat pants and cut off top showing off my toned abs. Although I may have been appealing to the eyes, I was broken and filled with pain on the inside. My eyes were still bloodshot from crying so hard earlier today. Yet, I managed to still find the courage to walk inside the office where everyone stood at attention. Smooth sat behind the

desk with Sweetz on his right and Kris and Krazy to his left. All eyes were on me as I walked into the middle of the room.

As always, Smooth was the first to talk. "So Samya the word is that you wanna leave the crew...Do you care to explain?" I looked Smooth dead in the eye before I responded. "This crew was formed and based on our ideas and when we wanted to take over the Downtown area and many other areas of the D, we made that happen together. But it seems that our partnership has changed and my talents and my rank in this crew got overlooked! I can't be a part of a crew where the loyalty shifts. Also my family died for no reason and it seems like no one in the crew wants to look into it, better yet even care."

Smooth stared back at me with no compassion before responding. "The death of your family is not the concern of the Hot Boyz. Clearly it was done because of your own personal issues." I was instantly in shock from his response. "What!? The murder of my family was not caused because of my personal issues!" "How sure are you about that?" Krazy interjected with a sick smile on her face. "I'm damn sure it's not because of my personal issues! And I appreciate it if you wipe that damn smile off your face while talking about the murder of my family!" I snapped.

Krazy began laughing hysterically. "What the fuck is so funny?" I spat out of anger. "You might call it murder but I call it sweet poetic justice! You sit around here claiming you a hit man but when it comes time to get your hands dirty you are sloppy as they come! Sweetz and I had to do double time to cover up your tracks! You are not worthy of the title hit man nor the name of the Hot Boyz." Krazy explained, filling me up with rage.

"Bitch I'm more than worthy to carry the title! You think just because you have a little bit of street cred that you can look down on me! If it wasn't for me you and Kris would still be on the streets selling them weak ass nickel and dime bags!" I yelled with anger.

<u>Krazy</u>

I stood there with my rage boiling up inside of me to the point I could no longer control it! I slowly walked away from Kris's side as I reached behind my back for my 9mm. If she thinks that she deserve some type of fucking medal because she introduced Kris and I to Smooth, then that bitch is sadly mistaken! Before Smooth, Kris and I was well known in these streets, and meeting Smooth was just a mothafucking plus in our book! If it wasn't for Kris and I putting in work, the Hot Boyz wouldn't be so Hot in these streets.

With a quickness, I walked to Samya, invading her space, and leaned forward to whisper in her ear. "That may be true.... but thanks to you, your family is burnt to a crisp because you didn't know how to keep your legs closed." I laughed. "I enjoyed hearing their pleading cries. it's just a shame they didn't know how much of a hoe you were. I bet they are turning in their graves..oops I forgot there are no graves because they're nothing but ashes!" I continued with nothing but a smile on my face. Yet, within seconds Samya pushed me with force, causing me to lose my balance.

I quickly pulled out my 9mm and aimed it at her ready to pull the trigger when she tackled me onto the ground. Samya was trying with all her might to get the gun out of my hands, but with quick thinking, I head-butted her, smashing into her nose and quickly pushed her off me. I got on top of her and began to beat her with the end of my gun till she was spitting out blood! Placing pressure onto her face, I opened her mouth and stuck the barrel my gun inside.

"You stupid bitch, you think you can kill a killer? I should pull this trigger and rid this world of your worthless life you bum bitch! You think I wasn't going to find out what you were doing in my sheets with my man? You think that I was going to sit here and let you get away with disrespecting me like that? " I yelled while I fed this bitch my gun.

Tears rolled down Samya's face as I pushed the gun further in her mouth. I just envisioned myself pulling the trigger and blowing that miserable bitch's brains all over the floor! How dare she sit here and cry but call herself a hit man! That bitch had balls enough to sleep with my man but scared to look death in the eye! Well today she going to meet her maker because I'm the grim reaper and I'mma take that bitch's soul!

"That is enough Krazy!!! Let that bitch go so she can get her sorry ass up out this establishment." Kris yelled, snapping me out my moment. I looked at Kris, and looked back down at the pathetic excuse of a woman. I hocked back and spat on her face before I decided to let her go. Samya was truly the scum of the bottom of my shoe, and I treated her as such. I sashayed back to the side of my man and looked the bitch dead in her eye's making a silent promise to myself that next time I will take that bitch's life.

The silence of the room was broken when Smooth stood up, placing his hands on the desk, and stared Samya in the eye. " Well, since everyone got what they need to say off their chest. I, Smooth, the leader of this crew dismiss you from all your responsibilities." He started, nonchalantly. "But know this, if we suspect any conspiracy against this crew...I will let Krazy finish what she started with no hesitation, and Kris won't be there to save you either. Now get the fuck up out my office!" Smooth finished with force.

Everyone stood there in silence as Samya pick herself up off the floor, and wiped the blood from her mouth. She glared at Smooth before exiting the room. The tension was so thick in the room that no one knew what else to say until...

"Well I'm glad that bitch is gone... You know good and well that bitch got on your nerves, even though she was fine as hell. Damn and a nigga didn't even get to hit it yet! I should've got my dick sucked at least!" Mike joked, causing us to all laugh. Out of all of us, Mike was the one to bring humor out of any serious situation with the Hot Boyz. Sometimes, we all needed that.

<u>Samya</u>

I limped back into my car, in pain from the inflictions on my body. Without hesitation, I pulled down the mirror to look at my face, only to see the bruises that began to appear. I took out a napkin and lightly dabbed the remaining blood that was on my face. I can't believe that bitch killed my family! All over a nigga that I haven't fucked in years!

My blood began to boil once again as I reached into my purse, pulled out my phone and called my brother J-ro. He was the only survivor out of my family, and right now he was my listening ear. Tears cascaded down my face as I yelled and vented to him through the phone.

"Smooth ain't do nothin' about it with his bitch ass. He just acted like it was ok. He never recognized my skills and was always praising Kris and Krazy for their shit. Doesn't he know that I was the one who put they ass on. Without me there would be no fucking Hot Boyz! And look at what they did? They shitted on me like I was nothing to they ass." I ranted, not letting J-ro get a word in. "That's alright 'cause they are going to get what's comin' to them. I'mma fuck they whole world up... Just watch!" I continued on the phone before pulling out of the spot. I was determined that from this day forward that shit was about to go down, and I would never be that bitch that gets played again.

CHAPTER 2: DRASTIC MEASURES

<u>Smooth</u>

Things have finally gotten back to normal as time progressed. Kris and I were back on the streets making moves, the Hot Boyz had full reign over the D, and we were getting ready to expand our territory. But that all came to a halt, when I got a call about an emergency meeting. By the time we arrived back at the house, we were five minutes late to the meeting. Although it may not seem that late to normal people, but to a "Hot Boy" it means a lot. Time is money, and money is time. When you're late, you're losing money, and when you're losing money, that means you're losing time left of your life.

Kris and I walked into the house where my sister, Tahliyah a.k.a Liyah, met up with us looking heated. Her smooth caramel brown skin was turning red with anger, her natural light brown eyes turned cold black, while her wavy black hair was now pulled back into a tight bun. From the looks of it, she was pretty pissed off. "Where the fuck have ya'll been?" Liyah interrogated, not giving us time to answer. "You know what, Fuck that! Just bring ya' asses on." She yelled, while heading upstairs. "What the fuck is wrong with you?" I asked while following her. Liyah sighed, "Look, we gotta new gang in the streets." "Oh please, they ain't gonna' last long." Kris laughed. "Keep thinkin' that." Liyah commented.

"What the fuck are you talkin' about Liyah?" I asked angrily. "Just wait until the meeting starts." She replied, while opening the double doors, revealing all of the "Hot Boyz" sitting at the table in the boardroom, including Krazy.

Liyah and Krazy were the only girls in our affiliation. We would not accept any other females because of the emotional baggage that comes along with them. Being in the Hot Boyz, there is no such thing as emotions. We take niggas out, and we run the cities we step in, so who has time for emotions? I scanned the boardroom to make sure every member was there. Pistol and Killa' Mike was there, followed by Flash, P.J, Jywan, Money, and Blade. Our affiliation was huge, but they were the real movers and shakers behind it all.

"Wassup fellas." Kris greeted, while sitting down. "What up." The crew greeted in unison. "Aiight let's get this straight, what's this shit about this new gang?" I asked, smoking a blunt. "Well..." Flash, the oldest member out of the crew at the age of 45, started to answer. "There's this new gang called H-Block, and they are starting to take over."

"Mmmhmm...So what?" Kris added. "Look they've been movin' ova' to every city, taking over all territories." Pistol explained. "And where are they from?" I asked, exhaling smoke. "They're from L.A." Replied my main man Money, who was damn near a splitting image of the rapper Nelly.

"Aiight, so why are we talkin' about them?" Kris asked in his hardcore manner. "They're taking over our territories." Killa' Mike exclaimed. "What?" I yelled angrily. I never had a problem with other gangs coming up...But when they fuck with my shit, that's when we have a problem.

"They have boys over here takin' over our territory." Mike started. "Our hoes, our clubs..." Blade continued. "Our drugs." Flash stated. "Our money." Money commented, and finally P.J filled in "Our everything."

I took a long gulp from my drink before I spoke again. "Aiight this is the plan, Flash you get the weapons, PJ you get the info, Money... You watch our drugs and our connects. Jywan, I want you to watch them hoes, the clubs, and the barber shops out here on these streets."

I turned and looked in the direction of Kris and Liyah. "Kris, Krazy, Blade, and Pistol, when you find them little punks, you kill their ass nice and clean. And Liyah, you make sure the money flow is tight...Ya'll got it?" I continued, before everyone agreed in unison.

"Ok, tomorrow at twelve we are having another meeting so until then....Peace." Liyah announced. "Hot Boyz for life."

Everyone ended in unison. The meeting was finally adjourned, and it was time for me to go to my room, and think of other ways to keep the Hot Boyz at the top.

While all the members left, I noticed Mike was looking heated, but I shook it off, and went to my room. As I sat on my bed, I slowly smoked my blunt filled with kush, to calm my nerves. This was my usual routine after having a meeting with the Hot Boyz, since it allowed me to meditate on shit. I closed my eyes and slipped into my "calm mood," when all of a sudden Mike busted in.

"That was some foul ass shit that you pulled Smooth." Mike yelled, ruining my peaceful aura. "What the fuck are you talkin' about? And who told yo' ass to bust into my room?" I snapped. Mike disregarded all that I just said, and continued to rant. "You gave all those niggas something to do...But I didn't get one damn thing to do." Mike started, "I know all about these niggas, and I would've got them lil' niggas straightened out." He continued.

"Yeah ok." I laughed, which made him even more mad. "You think this is a fuckin' joke? I'm your fuckin' blood! The least you could have done was let me be a part of this shit." Mike yelled. "I don't give a fuck if you're my blood or not!" I retorted. "You fuck shit up. And this shit is too hot to let you fuck that up." I finished. "Bullshit!" Mike replied, while punching my wall. "I don't fuck shit up. You just never give me a chance to show you what I'm about." "Please! All you're about is fuckin' some broads raw." I spat. "That alone shows me how irresponsible yo' ass is...You don't think shit through nigga." I explained.

"Fuck you Smooth! Just because you're the leader does not make yo' ass a God or some shit! You're just as fucked up as I'am." Mike said, with tears of anger falling down his face. "I might be. But I'm smarter, and better than yo' dumbass." I spat. "You're going to regret this shit bitch! Your ass is going to need me." Mike replied, while heading to the door.

"Yeah, and that will be the day that one of us die...And I'll be damned that it would be me." I said coldly, causing Mike to turn around and give me his infamous smirk. "Yeah ok nigga. You will wish you never said that." Mike calmly replied before he stormed out my room.

Something about that sentence hit me hard, yet I couldn't understand why. Fuck! Why do I have to go through this brotherly shit? All I try to do is to get him to grow the fuck up, but his ass will never learn. To calm my nerves once again, I sparked my blunt back up, and began to enter "my zone".

<u>**Introducing Mike:**</u>

Four in the morning, and here I 'am driving down Jefferson Ave, drinking my life away. From 1800 to Hennessey, I went through bottle after bottle while Lil Wayne blasted throughout my escalade. Smooth really knows how to get a nigga pissed off.

I need something else to get my mind off this shit. Liquor ain't hitting it. I need more than that...I need some ass! But from who? I'm tired of fucking all these little hood rats. I fucked women from the Eastside to the Westside of Detroit... Shit, even those who live in Ann Arbor and Lansing. It was the same ole, same ole, and it was getting tiresome. I need a new and sexy little thang, that can work me all night, and be what the rapper Plies call 'em...She can be my bust-it baby.

Just as I hit a red light, I spotted a sexy caramel girl sitting at the bus stop. I had to get her, so I rolled down my window, and greeted her with a "Heyyy."

"Hey." She replied with a smile. "Why are you at the bus stop ma? You know the bus stops running down here at this time right?" "My car broke down, and I'm here stranded." She responded, while getting close to my window. "You need a ride?" I asked genuinely.

"Well, I don't know..." She said hesitantly. "Aww don't be like that ma'. I won't bite unless you want me to." I joked, yet still trying to reel her in with my sweet smile. "Ok!" She laughed. Ha! I knew she couldn't resist me. I'm Killa' Mike. Who would turn me down? Let's be real, I'm cute, got money, got the clothes, the car, and I can make 'em laugh...Shit, I'm the man every girl wants.

Making her way to the other side of my car, she sat on the passenger side, and checked out the scenery while I drove off. "So what's your name?" The girl asked innocently. "Mike, and you?" "Keylo." She responded sweetly. "Ok, well you know Keylo, you are fine as hell." I said, while licking my lips. "Thanks." She giggled.

"How old are you?" I interrogated. "Sixteen and you?" "I'm seventeen baby girl." I answered with a huge smile. " Foreal? " She asked with a smile. "Reeeeeaaaaaal!" I said with a drunken slur, "You look older..." She started, but I quickly cut her off.

"Whatchu' tryin' to say? I look like an old man or some shit?" I joked. "No...Not with that baby face. You look like you're twenty-one." She continued. " Well shit, I still look good don't I?" I replied, while playfully checking myself out in the rearview mirror. "Yes you sure do." She laughed, not realizing that I parked in a vacant alley. It was time to stop the talkin', and time for the panties to be droppin'.

"You want to do somethin'?" I asked, while leaning towards her. "Like what?" Keylo asked nervously. With that I whispered nasty gestures in her ear, letting her know that I wanted to fuck. "Uhhhh...I don't think so." She interjected. "C'mon ma'...You know you want to." I said, while starting to kiss on her. "No...No I don't." Keylo said while trying to push me off. Too bad it didn't work. "Yes you do." I said while getting on top of her. "Please stop." She cried.

At that moment I snapped. One thing I hate more than anything, is a fucking tease. If she didn't want to fuck, then why step in my car? Why did she even let me take her ass to an alley? Is she dumb? I'm Killa' Mike, no girl turns me down.

"Bitch shut the fuck up." I yelled, while pulling a gun to her head. Keylo quickly sniffled and got silent. I ripped off her clothes and forced myself into her, causing her to cry harder. For hours, I took advantage of this girl, making her my sex slave. And when I was done with her, I dropped her off at an abandoned building. Not giving two fucks about what happened to her.

<u>Keylo:</u>

I watched as the baby blue escalade pulled off, leaving me at this abandoned building with not a strip of clothing. I never felt so weak and low until now. I had to get home.

Luckily, I found a pay phone with twenty-five cents next to it. With the little strength I had, I called my cousin. "Hello." His deep voice flowed over the phone. Even through my cries, I explained what happened.

"What car did this nigga drive Key?" My cousin angrily interrogated. "A baby blue escalade, with "MI Made" on his license plate. His name is Mike." I answered. "I swear I'm going to kill that nigga." My cousin responded. "Where you at?" He asked. I cried harder as I told him where I was. How could this have happened to me? " You just stay tight, I'm on my way." He quickly stated before hanging up.

Within ten minutes, my cousin Jayden pulled up in his all black Mercedes SUV. I hopped into the car, and changed into the clothes he provided for me. "Where are we going?" I asked, while observing the anger planted all over his face. "We are going to find that motherfucker and I'm going to gut him like a fish." Jayden replied coldly.

Some may think he is exaggerating, but in our family we mean what we say. So when he says that he will gut Mike, I knew he meant that from the pit of his stomach. Tonight was Mike's last night on this earth, and I hope his bitchass enjoyed it.

<u>Sweetz</u>

I was in my bed knocked out, when all of a sudden my phone rang. "Hello." I answered groggily. "Sweetz..." The voice of Smooth traveled through my phone and pierced my heart. Just from the tone of his voice, I knew something was wrong.

"What's wrong babe?" I asked concerned. "We need to talk...I'm downstairs." Smooth replied, disregarding my question. Without another word said, I jumped out my bed, and headed downstairs to the kitchen. Waiting for me at the backdoor was Smooth. It was pouring rain, but I could still see the tears strolling down his face. I grabbed his hand and pulled him into the kitchen. We sat at the table for about five minutes in silence until he spoke.

"M-M-Mike is dead." "What?" I replied in shock. "He got killed...They gutted him like a fish...You should have seen it Sweetz, it was blood everywhere... On the seats, over the dashboard. Blood...Was everywhere." Smooth stammered.

I grabbed his hand over the table, and as much as I tried to fight it, all I could do was cry. Why would anyone kill Mike? He was the sweetest boy I ever met. He was like everyone's little brother. Not only did Krazy and I take him in as our little brother, the whole community did.

"Who would do this to Mike?" I asked astonished. "I don't know...But I'm going to find that nigga and kill him...Just like he killed Mike." Smooth yelled in anger, while he jumped up and headed to the door.

"Smooth, where are you going?" I interjected. "I'm going to find the bitch that killed my brother!" He snapped. I ran in front of the door to stop him from leaving. "No Smooth!" "Move Sweetz!" Smooth commanded. "No...I'm not letting you go out there and do something stupid babe. You don't even know who did this to him, and I'm not letting you kill an innocent man out of anger Smooth. I love you too much to let you do that baby." I explained, while tears cascaded down my face.

This man just doesn't know how much I love him. If he wanted, he could have killed me on the spot for trying to stop him, but his love for me was so deep, that he would only allow me to stop him from getting his revenge. Knowing Smooth, no one can stop him from doing anything he is determined to do, not even his own grandma!

Interrupting my thoughts, Smooth stared into my eyes, dropped down to his knees and did something I never seen him do. He began to cry. I knew that this was hard on him. Mike was not only his little brother, he was his heart. I dropped down on my knees and held Smooth in my arms, while he cried on my shoulder. "It's all my fault." Smooth repeated over and over again. "No it's not Smooth." I opposed. "Yes it is!" Smooth snorted. He pulled away from me and looked into my eyes. "I told him that the day I would need him is the day he would die...That was the last thing I told him before he died. If we didn't argue, then he would still be alive...This shit is all because of me." Smooth explained.

"Baby....You said that out of anger, you didn't mean that. He knew that you loved him no matter what. And this isn't your fault. It was his time to go baby, as sad as it is...but it had nothing to do with you. And you have to stop beating yourself up over it...Ok?" I asked. "Ok..." Smooth sighed.

"Now come on. Let's get you out of these wet clothes and go to bed ok?" I suggested, while getting up off the floor. I offered him my hand, hoping that what I just said helped him, but Smooth just sat on the floor, and stared off into space. I knew this would mess with his mental. But out of the two of us, I had to be strong and keep him on track. After two minutes of being in his "own world", Smooth grabbed my hand for support off the ground, and followed me upstairs. I undressed him and took him into the shower.

The warm water was so inviting, yet was not enough to get Smooth out of his trance. His eyes were so cold and sad. After I washed him in the shower, I oiled him up, and laid next to him in my bed. His arms were wrapped around my naked body, letting me know that he was still here with me physically, but I knew he was mentally gone.

"I love you." Smooth softly spoke, just as I was dozing off to sleep. "I love you too baby." I replied, after I quickly turned around, and stared into his honey colored eyes. I wanted to kiss him so bad, but I knew this wasn't the time for that. Yet, Smooth must have read my mind, because he grabbed my face, and planted the most deep, and emotional kiss onto my lips.

This one kiss led into him on top of me, pumping in and out of my pussy ever so roughly. I laid there allowing him to take out all his emotions on me. The pain was pleasure to me, but to him this was just pain. To Smooth, there was no pleasure involved since he lost his brother.

He held my legs up in the air, and continued to thrust long, hard, and slow strokes. Each thrust was stronger, never missing my g-spot. Tears of pleasure and pain cascaded down both of our faces. After hours of hardcore sex, we both came in unison and fell asleep. Everything that we once knew was surely going to change. I knew that whoever killed Mike was asking for war, and Smooth was going to make sure of that.

Today is the day of Mike's funeral. Everyone, who was everyone was there. People traveled from L.A, New York, even Puerto Rico to come share their condolences to Killa' Mike. Everyone was at the Hot Boyz house, eating and drinking trying to lighten up from such a tragedy. Smooth was being a good host to all, while Krazy and I sat in the kitchen sipping on champagne "Girl, I don't know how things will be now that Mike is gone." Krazy commented, while staring at everyone mourning together in the living room.

"Yeah." I sighed. "Mike always kept things lightweight you know? He was always the one who kept us laughing...Now it's going to be more serious you know?" I finished in between sips of my champagne. Krazy's face became more serious after I made that comment. Why? I don't know, but it had to be something on her mind that was bothering her. "What's wrong girl?" I asked concerned. "Man, it's just that things are going to get more serious...It's going to be like the old days before Kris and Smooth left. Maybe worse." Krazy replied.

"What do you mean? Things weren't that bad before they left. That was when they were in their prime. You know Smooth and Kris making moves, doin' it big, takin' niggas out and runnin' shit." I exaggerated, with a smile at the thought that came to mind. The thought consisted of the money, cars, and clothes that were earned because of their affiliation. Yet Krazy wasn't feeling the same way.

"Yeah...The money, the cars, and all the other shit was nice. But the blood, sweat, and tears that was put into this shit, just to get us to where we are now ain't no joke. You only got a little glimpse of how shit goes down when Smooth and Kris was in Atlanta but you have no clue how it was in the beginning." Krazy continued to ramble on and on like a mad woman. Losing me at the no joke part! "I guess, but I'm just glad that I don't have to be involved in it no more. I can sit back and enjoy life like I did before Smooth went to Atlanta. " I interjected. "Too bad I can't say the same. I'd give anything to have a normal life like others, but I really don't have a choice as of now." Krazy said, before taking a shot of Remy.

Although Krazy was my girl, I knew there was something that she wasn't telling me. We never discussed her past before her and Kris became a part of the Hot Boyz , but whatever happened back then, I knew it was something that was keeping her from having that normal life that she always wanted. My thoughts were interrupted by an old friend that started to walk towards us.

Her name was Cashmere. Krazy and I both knew her from way back when we were fourteen. She used to be just like us. All until she met Big Meech, a huge drug lord who claimed that he wanted to "take care of her". Yet Krazy and I both knew that he wanted to put her on his team and turn her into one of his prostitutes. Since he was also a pimp! Cashmere was determined to get out of Michigan, despite my warnings. With no questions asked, she packed her shit up, moved to L.A, and never came back.

"Heyy!" Cashmere greeted while giving us a hug. "Hey Cash, how have you been?" I asked, while observing her attire. Knowing good and well that this is a funeral, why in the world is this girl dressed in a lime green dress, with those big, exaggerating grandma church hats? I mean the color accented her smooth chocolate skin, but this is not the place for all of that!

Out of all the years I knew her, this girl always tried so hard to get attention. I always knew she was envious of Krazy, and of course she couldn't give two fucks about me. She was as fake as they come, and I always kept my guard up with that bitch.

"I've been doing real good girl, Loving L.A you know?" Cashmere replied, interrupting my thoughts. "Oh really." Krazy commented. "Hell yeah girl!" Cash laughed. "You still fuck with Big Meech?" I asked, while sipping on my drink. "Oh no girl! Fuck him. I'm going to school, and I got a new man that treats me right. He is fine, got mad money, and he knows how to lay the dick downnnn." Cashmere exaggerated, causing everyone to laugh except for Krazy.

Krazy:

While everyone was laughing about how Cashmere's man can put the dick down, I was still thinking about Cashmere going to school. Out of all the years I known her, she never wanted to go to school. Shit, she never even made it out of middle school. Going to college was my goal and she knew that I wanted to go for Forensic science.

"So, what are you going to school for Cash?" I interrogated. "Oh...You know, Forensic Science." She replied nonchalantly. Oh Hell no! "Bitch, how the fuck are you going to school for forensic science, knowing damn well yo' ass can't spend one hour in a fuckin' classroom!" I yelled with slurring words, since my ass was drunk off that champagne. "Ugh! Why would you say something like that to me?" Cashmere scoffed.

"Bitch I can say whatever the fuck I want to say, to who I want to say it to...You fake ass bitch!" I yelled, throwing my glass at her. Too bad I was too drunk to have good aim. My mission was to get that head, but I ended up hitting the refrigerator, missing her head by two inches.

"Bitch are you crazy?" Cashmere yelled. That alone caused me to get in her face and show her how Krazy gets down.

<u>Kris</u>

As I sat on the couch, sipping on my E &J, so many thoughts clouded my head. With Mike gone, things were about to get more intense. His death made me realize that this fast life also causes fast deaths. Some people would like to stop gang banging, and go back to a having a clean and regular life. I can't lie, some days I wish I could stop and live right. Yet, the money, the cars, and having that power, keeps me with the Hot Boyz for life. Something about controlling shit just keeps me on a natural high. I live to control. Controlling is my life.

Smooth and I are similar when it comes to control. He's not as bad as me though. Smooth loves being the one to make sure everyone is taken care of, like he is running things. But me...I like being the king, making people bow down. I make females stay in their place, and I rule whatever is in my way. No matter what I do, and who I fuck on the low, Krazy has my heart and has been there since we were in the sandbox. Out of all of the sacrifices I had to make for her, from taking her in when she had nothing and nobody, to buying her a house and a car...She and I both know that she owes me her life, and therefore, she is mine. I own her.

The loud sound of shattering glass interrupted my deep thoughts. I heard yelling and screaming coming from the kitchen. Quickly looking in that direction, my vision was hindered by people blocking the view. Once I heard Krazy's voice, I instantly got mad.

I threw my glass onto the ground out of anger, causing silence to float over the room. The crowd parted like the red sea, and as soon as I locked eyes with Krazy, she knew that she had fucked up. "Pick this shit up." I yelled sternly. With no questions asked, Krazy ran over to me, and began to pick up my glass off the ground. Before she got up to leave, I grabbed her arm, pulled her closer to me, and whispered in her ear. "Take your ass in the room." She looked into my eyes, giving me an empty stare. So empty, it seemed as though she had no soul... Like she was dead. That look pierced my heart, but I wasn't going to let her take my control.

<u>Sweetz:</u>

I watched as Krazy left the kitchen of commotion, like it never even happened, just to go pick up the glass that Kris threw out of his hissy fit. I couldn't understand that. How can she come from just being the baddest, bossiest, hell raising bitch, and turn around two seconds later and be a scared victim of Kris's control?

I knew Kris since I was fourteen, and don't shit about him scare me and would make me act like how she does. It has to be something from their past that has her like this. Whatever it is, it has to be real deep.

"Wow." Cashmere said, sounding like a zoned out zombie. "Yeah." I replied. "That is crazy how she just flipped off the crazy switch, and turned into a whole different person when it came to

Kris." Cashmere continued.

"Yeah...I don't know how and why, cause Krazy can take his little skinny ass out easily...This shit just doesn't make any sense." I commented. "He just has so much...Power." Cashmere spoke in pure awe and amazement, as if she didn't hear what I just said. I swear some of these girls from Detroit got some serious issues. I mean damn I thought I was bad, but to lust after the power a man has over someone else, is a hot mess.

"I know that's right." Smooth said, coming out of nowhere. I jumped and turned towards him, with a look of surprise. It felt as if he knew what I was thinking. "Huh?" I asked with confusion. "I mean it's crazy how ya' girl can be a bad ass and turn around and be his little puppet the next." Smooth clarified. "Oh." I sighed " Yeah that is crazy...I just don't understand it." I stated.

"Me either...Cause you know good and well that Krazy can lay him out anytime she wants to." Smooth joked. "Hell yeah, she would probably do that shit tonight while he is sleep." I laughed. "Naw...Knowing Krazy, she would do that shit while he is wide awake. Might wait 'til he is in the shower, butt ass naked, and stab him in his shit...Like BIIIITCH! That's for making me pick up that glass off the floor nigga!" Smooth joked, mimicking Krazy's voice, causing us to all start laughing.

"You're such a goofball Smooth." Cashmere laughed, while slapping her hand on his muscular arm, in a friendly manner. I quickly shot her a look, letting her know that I wasn't having it. "Smooth baby, let's go check on your grandma from Puerto Rico." I suggested, changing the subject. "Oh yeah, poor thing probably sitting there all quiet. You know she can't speak a lick of English." He laughed. "Right." I agreed, taking his hand, and leaving Cashmere standing in the kitchen looking stupid. I always heard that Cashmere was good for taking someone's man, but she and I both knew that my man was not the one. I would quickly cut any female who tried me.

Krazy

"After all the shit I've done for you, you're going to come up into my house and embarrass me like that. This is a fuckin' funeral Simone, not a damn house party where you can act a damn fool and cause commotion." Kris yelled, while I sat on the bed watching him pace back and forward out of anger. "I-" I began, but was cut off by Kris yelling again. "I -fucking nothing Simone! This day is Mike's day. Not yours. What did I tell you about that shit?" I sighed before I responded. "I'm sorry Kris." I apologized unenthused. "That's my good girl." He emphasized, while rubbing on the side of my face. I loved how he tried to be all sweet to me, but sometimes I hated when he would snap, and talk to me like I was a child.

I had a feeling that when Kris was to come back, things were going to go back to the old ways. He would be in control, and I would have to do whatever he would ask of me. I mean, after all, I owed him my life. I knew Kris ever since I was one-years-old, we both lived next door to each other, so his family was like my family. Yet, that all changed when we turned eleven.

There was a big time drug lord who came to the area and would always give our parents drugs. He told them that these drugs would calm their nerves, relieving them from the stress that living in the hood would cause. Little did they know, they were his lab rats, which he used to experiment on his new concoctions of different drugs. He would mix cocaine and crystal meth, making it so powerful that they would lose their mind. Which they did! Our parents were so cracked out, Kris and I had to get out on these streets and do what we had to do to take care of home...I remember it like it was yesterday...

May 2000

It was the worst rainy day in Michigan. No one was supposed to be outside due to the severe weather, yet Kris and I was outside on the corner of the East side of Detroit. Not just any corner, we were on Mack Ave, also known as Murda' Mack. Many know of it, but have never been there due to their fear of getting murdered. But that didn't stop Kris and I from selling our dope. We stood in the pouring rain, in our matching red hoodies and sweatpants, ready to make more money.

"Babe it's getting late, you need to go home 'cause we got to go to school in the morning. And you know you've been fuckin' up in school lately." Kris suggested. "I know." I responded in my baby voice. "You don't want them to find out what's going on and what we are doing on the low. I don't want them to take you away from me. You know you're my heart girl!" Kris said while staring into my green eyes. Every time he said that I'm his heart, I just wanted to melt.

"Ok baby..." I answered. Kris grabbed me by my hand and pulled me closer to him. He looked deep into my eyes, before placing a sweet kiss onto my lips. "Now hurry up girl." Kris said while smacking on my booty. "Whatever boy!" I laughed before heading home.

As I walked into my house with a smile on my face, eager to see Kris tomorrow, I heard voices coming from the kitchen. "This is what we are going to do Bubba Joe...We are going to bust into Big Man's house, take that money and some of that crack." The voice of my mom echoed. "But Tawny, you know Big Man will kill us if we did that." My father, Bubba Joe replied in his thick southern accent. "But baby, we need that crack." My mother pleaded. "Yeah," my father sighed. "We do...So when are we going to do this?" He asked.

While trying to sneak closer to the kitchen and be nosey, I accidentally stepped on my Siamese cat named Gina, causing her to scream in pain.

"What the fuck!" My mother yelled, looking into my direction. "Simone take yo' little ass to bed." She continued to yell sternly. "Ok." I sighed, putting my head down while I headed into my pitch black room. I laid in my cold bed and slowly drifted off to sleep. Hours passed when I was finally awakened by somebody grabbing my mouth, and dragging me out the room. I entered the illuminated kitchen only to see my father on his knees with a gun pointed to his head by the infamous Big Man.

Big man was 6'4', 340 pounds, with a vanilla wafer complexion due to his Puerto Rican heritage. His jet black hair was pulled back into a ponytail, and his honey colored eyes was now cold and distant. "Please, please don't kill me." My daddy pleaded. "Shut the fuck up!" Big man yelled loudly.

Kris:

I had a feeling that something was wrong when I heard yelling coming from Simone's window. I hopped out my bed, and peaked out my window only to see my Uncle a.k.a Big Man, pointing a gun at Mr. Simmon's head. Next thing you know, Simone's mom was pushing Simone towards Big man while saying, "Here, take her! I know we took your money but her pussy is worth more than that." "Mama!" Simone cried in shock. "Shut up Simone." Mr. Simmons yelled, while still on his knees at gunpoint. "But I don't want to go sleep with him." Simone cried. "Shut the fuck up! You're going to lay down, you're going to take it, and you're going to like it damnit." Mrs. Simmons said firmly.

I couldn't believe my eyes, they were going to give my baby girl away and let my uncle take her virginity. I quickly grabbed my pistol from under my bed, placed it in my boxers, and made my way over to the house. I snuck in through Simone's bedroom window, which was always left open for me and crept closer to the hallway.

I stood and watched for a minute since her Siamese cat, Gina, was attacking Big Man's leg. "Fuck this stupid ass cat!" Big Man snarled. Grabbing the cat by the tail, Big Man threw Simone's cat in the air. With the cat high in the air over Simone's head, Big Man shot the cat right in the stomach. Millions of pieces scattered all over the room and blood landed all over Simone. The look of shock and sadness hovered over Simone's face. From that alone, I couldn't take it.

I ran into the kitchen and started shooting. Big Man was first, then I shot Mr. and Mrs. Simmons, for the foul shit that they tried to pull on my baby girl. Simone sat on the ground crying harder and harder each second. I couldn't stand to see my baby girl cry.

I ran over to her, pulled her into my arms, and allowed her to cry on my shoulder. All while I began to calmly speak to her. "Don't worry baby I'm going to take care of you, and I won't let anybody ever, ever, hurt you again. You know you're my heart girl." I meant every word I said, and I knew that it was my obligation to take care of her from now on.

2004

Four years has passed, and now Simone and I are living in our own house on the Westside of Detroit. The Hot Boyz affiliation was just starting to take off on these streets. All we had to do was take out the AK47 boys, and we would officially be the lead gang taking over Detroit. Hot Boyz becoming the new gang meant more territory, more work, and even better...More power.

Smooth and I became cool ever since he moved up here from New York, and I met him through Samya. Smooth was different than the others out here trying to make a dollar. He was smart, and because of him, he introduced me into a new lifestyle.

This was the lifestyle of having others work under us as the movers and shakers, while we were the masterminds behind what we call a "business." This would be a sure fire plan, but first I had to take out the main crew of the AK47 boys. I had to kill them all by myself, and tonight would be the night. Simone and I sat in front of Saks bar and grill, waiting for them to come out so I can spray them down. I haven't done anything like this since I took out my Uncle and Simone's family four years ago. Sweat perspired down my forehead, while fear crept over me. I could see the six men coming out the bar. It was now time to do my job, but wait...What if they have a gun? What if one of them shoots back and killed us instead? What if?

So many thoughts clouded my mind, while I heard Simone's voice from the background. "Kris here they go!" She said. "Kris, get the gun!" "Kris...what the fuck are you doing ?" Next thing I knew, Simone grabbed my Automatic Handgun and started spraying all six of them before my eyes. It all happened so fast, I just sat there in pure amazement. How could she do this and laugh about it?

"Did you see that shit?" She laughed. "I got that nigga right there in-between his eyes. Brains were flying all over the place!" She exclaimed, in pure enjoyment. This chick was seriously crazy. "Girl, you're crazy...You know that?" I asked in shock, while we were speeding down the highway. She looked at me with a huge smile. "Ooo...I like that. That is going to be my new nickname. Crazy...But not with a 'C', Krazy with a 'K'... Since I'm a part of you Kris." She commented. Happiness gleamed all over her face while we drove home. From that day on, I knew that Simone was now going to be "Krazy" my new hit man.

Krazy:

After the day we took out the AK47 crew, Kris and I worked together when it came to his Hot Boyz business. I mean after all he did for me, I owed him my life. Whatever he would ask of me, I would do with no questions asked. I loved Kris with all my heart. He was my lover, my best friend, and more importantly he was my family. Without Kris, I had no one else, well that was before I met Sweetz at school.

It was 2004, my freshman year in high school. I sat in the lunchroom by myself, since I trusted no one, male or female. That all changed when I spotted her. She was a small brown skin girl with her hair in cornrows, glasses that looked like mine, and was weeping low self-esteem. From what I seen, she looked like she had a lot of pent up frustration.

It was something about her that reminded me of myself. I had to get to know her, I felt like I had to take her into my life. Making my way over to her, I sat next to her and greeted her with a simple "Hey". A simple hey became the start of a wonderful friendship that flourished on this beautiful day. Being around her made me feel like I was going to be able to have a normal life. To have a real friend that I had a strong connection with, a boyfriend who loves me, and to be able to go to school like a normal teenage girl, was truly a dream.

It was time to snap back to reality as I headed home from school, in my black caprice classic. I pulled up in front of my house only to see Kris sitting on the porch in a black hoodie that almost covered up his baggy pants, with the crispy black Air Force One sneakers. Whenever he was dressed in black, I knew it was time to make a move. We had a job to do, so there was no time to play.

I sat there in the car as he walked towards me, flashing me that sexy grin, and hopped into the passenger side. "What's good?" Kris greeted, while looking me up and down. I wanted to jump his bones right then and there, but I had to keep my composure, since we had business to handle. "Nothin'... So what's up?" I asked while staring into his eyes. The serious expression swept over Kris's face before he spoke. "I found out some info on that pussy ass nigga Quick. He is the leader of the AK47 boyz, and is the only thing that is preventing us from making that real money."

"Man, what I would do to kill that motherfucka' " I spat. "Don't worry mami you're going to have your chance to get this little bitch tonight!" Kris replied, causing a smile to creep over my face. "Good...I've been waiting on this shit." I said in excitement. "Yep. Now go cruise down to the Westside." Kris commanded, as he chilled back in his seat. Without another question asked, I pulled off and headed to the Westside.

The whole ride was silent until he told me to ride down Trinity Street. I slowly rolled down the street, until I spotted a whole bunch of guys chillin' at this one house. Kris quickly began to point out one of them to me. "You see that high yella' motherfucka' with the fitted on?" "Yeah." I answered, while taking a glance at the guy. "That's Quick. Your assignment tonight is to *fuck him, get info, kill him, and leave no evidence." Kris explained coldly. "Okay." I replied, while turning down another street that led me down onto the highway. Within ten minutes we were back at our house, plotting on how to take this bitch out.*

"I want you to go and get sexy for this party tonight where you will have to go and do your work." Kris explained as we headed upstairs into our bedroom. "Ok baby." I agreed. "Now you're going to have to fuck him, but I don't want you let your emotions get into this shit ok?" He asked while staring straight into my eyes, yet it felt like he was staring straight into my soul. I nodded my head in a trance, causing him to laugh his cute baby laugh.

"And one more thing..." Kris stated. "What?" I asked, finally getting impatient of standing. Kris continued to stand there, looking me over seductively before walking up and aggressively sucking all over my neck. I moaned lowly as I felt his hard dick pressing into my pussy. He started to suck on my ear while whispering "I got to get you loose for the business you're about to be doin' ok?" I nodded my head yes, as he ripped my sweats off, picked me up, and pent me up against the wall.

He held me with one hand, and with the other he pulled down his basketball shorts. With one quick thrust, he popped my cherry. This was my first time having sex, since I was still a virgin. Tears started to flow from my eyes as he pumped in and out of me furiously. I started to finally moan as he went deeper and deeper into my pussy. He gripped my hair, and continued to pump faster and faster as my juices started running down my legs.

I dug my nails into his back as he started to hit my g-spot, causing me to scream his name as I felt a warm sensation come over me and my body began to shake. I never felt like this before. More of my sweet juices flowed down my legs, as he passionately kissed me, and let me down. "Damn that shit was too good baby." Kris sighed, while rubbing his dick as he walked back into the bedroom. "Hell yeah." I laughed while following him.

"We are going to have to do that more often!" I joked. "Of course baby, now let's go take a shower." Kris replied, before walking up to me and kissing me passionately. Slipping his tongue into my mouth, he started gripping on my ass, causing my pussy to instantly get wet again. I would love to have a round two, but there was business that needed to be handled. I ended the kiss, grabbed his hand, and led him into the bathroom.

After our shower, I oiled up with my edible cherry flavored body oil, and slipped into my dress... with no underwear! This wasn't any old dress; this was a tight black strapless dress that stopped at my mid-thigh. When I say tight, I mean it was so tight that you could see my curves from a block away. It felt like my ass was about to fall out the bottom of my dress! I quickly walked into my room and started to put on my open toed stiletto heels that laced around my calves. After I finished lacing it up, I took a piece of ribbon and tied it around my thigh, to prevent exposure, and slid my blade under the ribbon. I grabbed my car keys and gave Kris a peck on the lips goodbye.

Unfortunately, before I could even walk out the front door,

Kris threatened me by saying, "Look you said you were down and all, but if I find out that you ain't do what you had to do, I'm goin' to leave yo' ass toothless!" With that in mind, I hopped into my car and soon enough I was back on the Westside.

Anxiety crept over me when I pulled up to the house. I swear I was about to piss on myself! There was nothing but nigga's there, and I swear I was the only female there with the exception of the few hoes. I slowly parked around the corner and strutted back to the party. I walked up in there with all eyes on me, but that wasn't stopping me from completing my mission. I looked around for my victim, but he was nowhere to be found in the living room area. I walked into the kitchen to get a drink when he walked in stumbling. Good, he was drunk!

I observed every detail of him. He was wearing black Dickies pants, a white tall tee, with his left sleeve rolled up to show his tattoo that had a picture of a sad clown and a happy clown with words that said " Laugh now Cry later." His fitted hat was tilted to the left side and a toothpick hung out the corner of his mouth.

I gazed at him as he flowed through the kitchen and straight to the dance floor. I quickly grabbed my drink, and walked into the living room where everyone was freaking the hell out each other. I slowly switched my hips over to the couch where he was sitting, and I stood right in front of him.

To appeal him, I began to rub my thigh up and down slowly, yet seductively. "What's good wit ya' mama?" Quick asked while licking his pink lips. "Shit, I was wondering the same thing about you." I replied in a sexy voice. "Shit chillin', you know what I mean." Quick smiled. Just then Play-N-Skillz song "Freaks" came on. "Do you dance ma'?" Quick asked, staring into my green eyes.

"Yeah but the question is do you?" I replied while licking my lips. "How about you find out." He smiled. I lead my way to the dance floor, as he followed my ass like clockwork. I slowly started to grind my hips to the beat as he licked his lips.

Finally getting tired of standing there and watchin' my ass move so seductively, Quick gripped me by waist pulling me closer to him, and started to dance with me. I looked deep into his eyes as I turned around, bent over to the front, and touched my toes. The harder I twerked him, the harder his dick got. As the song slowly faded, he held my hand leading me back into the kitchen and started to pour me a drink. "Damn mama, you got a nigga on hard and shit." Quick commented with a smile, causing me to laugh. "What can I say I just got it like that, you know what I mean?" I said while seductively leaning on the counter. Quick looked at me up and down before responding. "Yeah, most girl's don't know how to work their shit right, like they're a virgin or something."

I pulled him by his collar so that he could be in my face. "Well I am not like them hoes out there." I said, while nodding my head towards the living room. "I noticed that when you bent over and touched them toes… Making that ass clap for me." He smiled. Getting close to his ear, I began to whisper in a seductive tone. "Well if you like I can show you how that ass clap personally." "Aww shit I got me a freak!" Quick exaggerated.

"Yeah, but first we got to play a game." I continued. "Aight then."
He agreed, blindly entering the dangerous trap that I've set up for
him.

Introducing Quick:

I stood there and looked at ole' girl as she grabbed the
whole 5th of gin and grabbed my hand. I followed her all the way
into the back room, and sat on the couch as she shut the door
and astraddled my lap. "Okay this game is called 'You wish you
can touch'." She started, while lightly grinding on my stiff dick.
"Aight." I quickly replied.

"The rule is that whateva' I do to you, you can't touch me,
and if you touch me, you have to tell me a top-secret thing about
you." She explained. "Aight." I agreed. I sat back on the couch
and looked at her as she stood up, downed some of the gin, and
started to strip off her clothes.

I slowly slipped my hand into my pants and started to stroke
my dick as she started to rotate her hips, and stripped until she
was butt ass naked. She astraddled my lap once again, and
started to grind on me while sucking on my neck. Pulling my
hand out my pants, she replaced it with her hand, causing me to
tilt my head back as her soft angelic hand stroked up and down
my dick. She was stoking me so good, that my hands started to
tremble! I wanted to grip her round, apple bottom ass so bad, but
I couldn't. I almost nutted as she slid off my lap, pulled my dick
out, and just popped it in her mouth like it was a lolli-pop.

My hands gripped the back of her head, forcing her to deep throat my dick, when all of a sudden she stopped with a wide grin on her face. She stood up in front of me, with that tempting body, and shook her index finger side to side.

"Nah uh baby boy, you can't touch, so you have to tell me something about yourself." She said while a smirk. "I'm part of the AK47 boyz." I said while gripping my dick and stroking it. "Okay I got me a thug huh?" She smiled. "Yep!" I smiled back, revealing my one dimple.

Krazy:

After he told me his one fact, I started to pour him drink after drink until that nigga was pissy drunk. His lips were too loose and he would not stop telling me all his information about the AK47 boyz. When I got all I needed to know out of him, I stood up ready to leave. Kris's voice popped into my head "Fuck them and kill them."

I sighed before leaning on the wall, planting one foot on the arm of his chair, and started to play with myself while looking deep into his eyes. I started to moan loudly when out of nowhere, he came up to me and rammed his hard dick into my throbbing wet pussy. He gripped my waist as he plunged deeper and deeper.

I grabbed a whole handful of his hair as he continued to pump in and out of me. His body began to shake rapidly, so I quickly pulled him out of my pussy, and started to suck his dick until he nutted down the back of my throat. That's when I quickly slipped out my blade, and cut him right by his dick and his ball sack. He screamed loudly, as he hit the floor holding his damaged privates.

I sat on top of him and held the blade under his Adams apple. "Nigga your fuckin' with the Hot Boyz." I said coldly. "Man, I don't know what you talking about." Quick cried. He started whining like a little baby, but I wasn't hearing it. "Well, let me jog yo' memory." I replied with a smirk, before I slit his throat and poured the rest of the gin all over his body.

Taking the black lighter out his pocket, as well as a black and mild blunt, I lit the blunt, and took a puff. I looked over his body before rummaging around the room, searching for the items that I need to finish him off. When I found what I was looking for, I took the box of matches that were out on the table, struck a match, and threw it on his lifeless body as made my exit like nothing happened.

Feeling accomplished, I pulled up to my house and walked straight up to the room where Kris was. "I did it." I said calmly. Kris choked on his spit. "You did?" He asked. "Yep. I lit him on fire!" I exclaimed. "Aww shit...You're on that hot boy shit!" Kris leaped up, getting all hype. "Hell yeah baby..." I started, but the thought of him threatening me earlier tonight hit me. "But I did it cause you threatened me..." I continued sadly.

"I only did it for you." Kris replied, while getting close to my face. "How the hell are you doing it for me?" I said while starting to cry. *"That shit really hurt me baby."* I finished. *"I'm sorry baby, but I did that because of this..."* Kris said while pulling out a suitcase filled with money.

"Is that mine baby?" I asked while wiping my eyes. *"Yeah."* Kris said with a smile. I jumped up and hugged him. *"Thank you so much baby!"* *"I will do anything for you girl."* Kris said, while holding me tighter in his arms. *"I love you. You're my heart girl and you know that."* Kris continued, looking into my eyes. *"I love you too Kris..."*

All of my thoughts from my past with Kris were interrupted when Cashmere busted into our room, without even knocking. I swear this bitch is so rude. "Oh my bad." She giggled. "You're cool ma'...Wassup?" Kris asked while licking his lips. "Oh well, Sweetz needed Krazy to help her with the chicken." Cash explained. "Chicken?" I asked unenthused. "Yeah." She replied. "You busted into our room because of some chicken..." I began, but was cut off by hearing Sweetz yelling. "Krazzzzzzy! I need you." That was my cue to hurry up and help my friend. With quickness, I hurried down the stairs to the kitchen, leaving Cashmere and Kris in the bedroom.

Kris

I watched as Krazy hurried out the room to go help her girl Sweetz. That was what I admired about my girlfriend, no matter what went on, Krazy would always be there for those she loved dearly. That was rare to find in some females these days. The majority is all money hungry and is only in it for themselves. They can give two fucks about the one who has the title of being their so-called "man." Speaking of those types of females, Cashmere was the main one.

She has always been in my face since we were fourteen, and would not leave my ass alone for nothing. Yeah, I gave her the "D" every now and then, but to me she is nothing but a knock off Krazy. I peeped game from the beginning that ole' girl was envious of my baby. It killed her not to have anything similar to Krazy. Too bad she didn't have a clue on what my babygirl was doing to get the finer things in life. Krazy was a ride or die gangsta' bitch, while Cashmere was a scared, little girl. A real goon like me can peep game as soon as I talk to a person for five minutes alone. Being in the Hot Boyz, you have to be able to read people like the back of your hand. First rule of this world is to Trust no one!

"Kris!" Cashmere interjected. "Yeah ... wassup?" I said, snapping out of my thoughts. "I missed you baby..." Cash stated while heading over to me. "Yeah, I know you did." I replied with a chuckle. "Whatever, with your cocky ass." She laughed. "You know how I 'am...that is never going to change." I said, while staring into her natural dark brown eyes, which were now covered with green contacts.

"It's just something about you that I love...I think it's how much power you have." She explained while standing over me. I couldn't help but smile. For one chick that I couldn't stand, she sure knew how to stroke my ego. "That's good to know ma' " I said with a smile. "Mmmhmm." She said, while rubbing my shoulders and getting real close to my ear. I closed my eyes irritated at her whispering in her annoying, squeaky, baby voice. "Now that I'm back in town, hopefully you will have more time for me." I continued to sit there, thinking how this bitch was just clueless. I took a deep breath before replying.

"Well sexy, I wish I did...But I'm going to be real busy with the Hot Boyz." A look of pure hurt covered Cashmere's face. "But...I' am going to need you to do something for me though." I said, while looking deep into her eyes. A heart filled smile began to slowly creep over her face, just from me saying that I needed her to do something for me. Wow...How could she be so desperate to get played?

"You know I will do anything for you baby." She squealed with happiness. I gently grabbed her face and softly planted a long, passionate kiss onto her lips. The kiss quickly ended when the door flew open, only to reveal Krazy. "Man, tell me why this silly bitch burnt up all the damn chicken!" She laughed.

Krazy:

I stopped in the middle of my laugh when I noticed how close Cashmere was to Kris's face. I mean their face was like too close for comfort! Cashmere slowly turned around and looked at me with that fake ass, cheesy smile plastered on her face. The nerve of this bitch!

"Girl I got some good news!" I looked her up and down before mimicking her voice. "Really, like 'Oh My Gosh' what's the good news Cash?" She quickly rolled her eyes before replying, "Seriously Krazy. We were just talking about how it would be a good idea for you and Sweetz to come back to L.A. with me." I looked at her so unenthused. "That sounds exciting and all Cash, but I have to pass on that one."

Before Cashmere could say anything, Kris's deep voice filled the room. "On some real shit Krazy hear her out, cause think 'bout it, Smooth and I are going to be on some real hot shit since Mike is gone, and we can't take the chance of ya'll getting hurt. You feel me." He looked at me with those piercing grey eyes of his, causing my heart to sink into the pit of my stomach. I swear he just got back from Atlanta, and then wham- bam-damn, here he go trying to ship me off to L.A. with this fake bitch!

"You know what Kris, fuck it then! You want me to go to L.A. then that's what the fuck it's goin' to be then. You come back in town like you're the motherfuckin' King Tut trying to control everybody's life." I yelled while walking into the walk-in closet, grabbing a suitcase and throwing my clothes in violently.

"Like what the fuck Kris? Everything I've done for you! Everything I gave up just doesn't amount to shit in your eyes huh? Do you know what the fuck I went through when you left me the first time Kris? Well let me fill you in on a little something-something motherfucka' " I yelled, walking back into the room with my suitcase in one hand, and pointing my finger in his face with the other hand.

"I bet yo' black ass didn't even realize that when you left me, I was fuckin' pregnant with yo' mothafuckin' seed! I was so depressed and so stressed out, I ended up havin' a miscarriage, and where was Kris? You was down in ATL livin' it up, while you left me out here struggling and fighting these streets by myself!" I started.

"And you have the mothafuckin' nerves to ship me off like some damn secret! Fuck you mothafucka'... Talking that shit that you love me, that I'm yo' heart, but far as I'm concern nigga you don't have a heart!" I started to choke up while saying the last part of my sentence.

The tears started to form in my eyes, but I did not want him or that bitch Cashmere to have the pleasure to see me cry. I grabbed my shit, stormed out the room, and headed down the stairs. I heard Sweetz yelling after me, but I just didn't want to hear anything that anyone had to say anymore. As I was about to head to my car, I spotted Kris's all black Mercedes, with chrome rims and presidential black tinted windows. A smirk came across my face as I dug in my purse, searching for the copy set of keys to his car. I unlocked that bitch, and skirted out the driveway heading towards the store to pick up a pack of cigarettes.

Kris:

I watched as Krazy took off, in not her car, but in my fucking Mercedes! This was the first time I felt so lost, so vulnerable, and so weak. I think I Lost Krazy, something that I could never allow to happen...but today it did. I stared out the window while a single tear cascaded down my cheek. I lost her, and I lost our baby. This was too much at one time.

"Baby, are you ok?" Cashmere asked in her cheesy voice. "Leave me the fuck alone!" I said coldly. "But..." She continued but was cut off by me yelling. "Get the fuck out hoe!" Without a word said, she walked out and left me in my room. Damn...I didn't think that this minor suggestion would hurt my baby so much. I was too busy thinking about me and what's the next move that I'm going to make, I never thought twice about how my babygirl felt. The abrupt knock on my door interrupted my deep thoughts.

"Who is it?" I asked in annoyance. "Smooth." The deep voice answered. "Come in." I sighed as I sat on the bed. "What the fuck just happened here man?" Smooth interrogated, while taking a seat in the chair across my bed. I explained everything that just happened, all while silent tears fell down my face.

I was never one to cry, but damn...losing my baby girl, and losing my power is something that I can't cope with. "Damn Kris... This is not the time to lose your girl over bullshit!" Smooth commented. "I know." I sighed. "But I actually think it's best for us to split. I need time to think shit through." "What! Nigga are you serious? You're going to let her go, after all of this? She is your down ass ride or die. She is your heart. And you're going to let her go?" Smooth exclaimed in shock. "Well a nigga has to do what he has to do." I replied coldly.

As of today, the Kris and Krazy saga is over. It's my time to shine and have more power. I'm just going to have to do shit without her. All I have to do is get rid of those who are preventing me from gaining more power. This is a one man job. She was my hit man, but I have to do this shit myself. So back to my plan, one down, one more to go...

__Smooth__

After Mike's funeral, the Hot Boyz affiliation has become more intense than it ever has. The crime, drug sales, and killing rate has increased. That new H-block gang is our biggest rivalry. They have even tempted some of our own men to be a part of their crew! Too bad I had my hit men lay all of the traitors out. I can't slip up and let the weaklings tell our secrets to the enemy. They had to die.

Trusting people in the Hot Boyz has become a hard thing to do. I don't know who the fuck to trust. Money can be the root of all evil, and in this world it really is. Friends are really foes, foes can never be your friends, and the ones you love can't even be trusted. I knew this before I entered this world of corruption, but now I'm really facing this shit.

I sat in the dark office area of my secret apartment in Lansing, thinking of my next move. I was always ten steps ahead of them, which was the only thing that kept me alive. People may think that I'm just going with the flow, not thinking twice... But I was the mastermind of it all. I made the Hot Boyz who they are today, and I will be damned to let anyone fuck that up. I sipped on my E &J and pondered over what I was going to do next.

As the saying always goes, "Drastic times cause for drastic measures." In order to keep the Hot Boyz from falling under, I had to make a drastic move. Shit is getting harder every day, but we are just going to have to grind harder, move faster, and do things better. My father always told me to not only think about the next move, but to think about the next five moves.

Most of my moves were going to consist of our drug supply that was coming from Columbia. Unfortunately, those who were playing the role as the middleman were getting corrupted by the enemies, and as a result were getting killed off because they knew too much. I can't risk losing our connects because of weak links getting turned out by the enemy. If I lose my connects, then I will lose everything. So to get rid of the trouble, I'm going to have to pull an 'American Gangster' move, I'm going to have to take my ass down there and get my supplies myself!

I grabbed my backup minute phone and called Liyah. "What's up?" She answered. "I came up with a decision tonight." I said in a serious tone. "Ok, fill me in on it." Liyah said, giving me all her attention. "Tomorrow night, I will head to the Columbia on my private jet and handle some serious business." "Ok do you want me and Kris to go with you?" Liyah asked, out of instinct.

"No." I coldly replied. "I'm going by my damn self! Too much shit is going on. I need you to hold it down and be on the lookout for me. You will be the only one who will know that I'm leaving to get the supplies." I explained. "But what about Kris? Or Sweetz? Or the Hot Boyz?" Liyah asked in pure confusion. "What about them Liyah?" I yelled angrily.

"They don't need to know shit. Just tell them I had to go out of town for family shit. You know the rules. You can't trust anyone. Not even the one you love Liyah.... But blood is thicker than water. So even when all these motherfucka's turn on us, we are all we got. Since Mike is gone sis, it's just me and you. Who can look out for us other than us?" I said, reminding her of our reality.

"Right." Liyah sighed. "But Sweetz is your girlfriend." She continued, hitting a soft spot in my life. "I know. I told her I wasn't going to leave her, but shit business goes before love. Drastic times cause for fuckin' drastic measures you know? So I will handle that on my own." I started.

"All I want you to do is hold it down for me. Be my eyes, and fill me in on everything. Every minor detail...Let me know. I will be gone for a while. My servant Pedro will come in late at night and fly in the supplies every now and then. You have to get them and hide them in the black hole. You know what I'm talkin' about. Don't sell it, don't do shit. Make it seem like we have a drought so we can break the Hot Boyz and see who is corrupt and who is legit. Then when I come back we will handle that shit. The main priority is to kill off H-Block. Let them be the man on the street, and then we come in for the kill. Shit is going to change big time for the Hot Boyz, but I told you we from the beginning, we all we got!"

"Right Smooth, we all we got. I will get on it tonight. I'm going to call Pedro and tell him that he needs to get the jet ready for tomorrow night." Liyah replied, telling me just what I was about to ask of her. That was the thing about Liyah, she was always on her shit and would never let me down. Liyah was my backbone, the one who helped me create this success, and the one who will be there for me in the end. "Thanks Liyah, I love you sis." "Love you too bro...I'll hit you up lata'. "She said before hanging up. Now that I have the business moves planned out, it's time to work on my next move...My love life.

<u>Sweetz</u>

Gucci Mane's "Vette Pass By" blasted throughout my loft, while I danced around in my pink boy shorts and white cami, rapping the words to the song. I just had three cups of my Pink Panty dropper concoction and I was feeling too good.

"Dance with me Mr. Giggles." I said while picking up my golden retriever puppy, and bounced around the couch. Other than Smooth, Mr. Giggles was my heart. I loved that puppy like it was a child I birthed myself. No matter what went on in my life, I could always come home and cuddle up with my puppy.

I continued to prance around my loft with Mr. Giggles, until I heard a knock at my door. "Who the fuck would come over here at four in the morning?" I spoke out loud while opening the door, only to see Smooth standing there. One glance at him and I instantly got turned on.

With his hair freshly braided in cornrows, Smooth wore dark blue baggy jeans, a fitted white short sleeved shirt with a black Gucci blazer over it, and some black Gucci leather loafers. The scent of his Chrome cologne thrilled my senses, and the sight of the bouquet of pink roses in his hand brought a huge smile across my face.

"Baby, what are you doing here?" I asked in pure shock. "I came to see you baby." Smooth replied in his sexy voice. "Mmm, well come in." I said as I grabbed his hand and led him into my loft. After I sat the flowers on my kitchen counter, I fixed my baby his favorite drink, which was rum on the rocks, and cuddled up with him in the couch. Day 26 played throughout my loft, setting the mood for the late night. "Baby I have something that I've wanted to talk to you about for a while now." Smooth started, staring intensely in my eyes. "Ok baby." I said, in a soft voice, patiently waiting for him to speak.

"From the very moment I first laid eyes on you, I knew you were the woman I wanted to take lead in my life. I love everything about you. We shared so many special times together. You were there for me when shit was going down, and even when I left to go to handle business, you could've went and fucked with some other lame ass guys, but you stayed faithful to me!" He started.

"You are my heart La'nay. You've seen me at my weakest moments where I all I could do is just cry, and you would just hold me in your arms, and give me all the love and support that I need. I can't picture me with no other female! And I'm for damn sure not going to lose you." Smooth explained, causing my heart to melt.

One thing about Smooth, when he opens up and gets transparent with you, that meant that he really loves you, and wanted to take things to another level. Something at the pit of my stomach churned, causing me to sit up and get prepared for what is going to come. I knew tonight was going to be special, or it could be the end of us!

Smooth quickly got off the couch, and got in front of me on bended knee. Tears instantly fell just at the sight of Smooth on bended knee. My baby was actually proposing to me! Pulling the little blue Tiffany's box from his pocket, Smooth presented a pink, 6.5 carat diamond ring. I couldn't believe my eyes, for a moment like this, all I could do was cry.

"La'nay." Smooth started. "You are my heart, you are my backbone, and you really are my queen. I want to wake up to you every morning. I want to come home and make love to you every night... And to get to that goal, I want to take the first step and make you my wife. So right now, on bended knee I'm asking you La'nay Jenkins to marry me...So will you marry me?" He continued, with a single tear flowing down his soft cheek. "Yes! I will marry you Rico Vasquez." I cried out, calling him by his government name. Smooth placed the beautiful ring on my finger, and pulled me into his arms as we cried together in pure joy.

"I want to make a baby tonight." Smooth whispered in my ear. I pulled away and stared into his eyes. "Are you serious baby?" I asked. "Yes. You never know what will happen to me being a Hot Boy and all, but I want to make sure I leave some part of me on this earth. I want to have a baby with you and only you. Our first child!" He exclaimed with a huge smile. "So let's go half on a baby tonight." He suggested.

I took a second to think. As much shit this man has been through with me, as much as he done for me, the least I can do is give him the one thing he asked me for... A baby! "Ok let's do it!" I squealed while hugging and kissing him one more time.

Before I knew it, I was in the doggy style position, with Smooth pumping slow and rough inside me. R. Kelly's "Half on a baby" blasted throughout my loft as Smooth grabbed my throat with one hand, and rubbed on my clit with the other, all while fucking me deeply from the back.

Our hands were entwined, as sweat was dripping off of him onto me, and I loved every minute of it. This was the best sex of my life. Pulling his thick dick out of my pussy, Smooth smacked the head of his dick on my clit, leaving me begging for more. "Mmm...Give me that dick baby." I moaned. "You love daddy's dick huh?" Smooth whispered in my ear. "Yes daddy." I moaned as he rubbed on my clit.

"Mmm...I want you to have my baby. Make me a real daddy." Smooth said while rubbing his dick on my pussy. Just from that alone I began dripping. "Ok baby," and with that said, Smooth thrusted his manhood inside of me and fucked me like no other, all while whispering Spanish into my ear. After a long round of pleasure, we came in unison, creating our new baby.

After our night of making love, Smooth went out of town to handle some family business. Ever since his father died, Smooth was the one who took care of his family. I knew that family was important to him so I couldn't blame him for going to take care of the issues that were ruining his family.

Before he left, Smooth placed all of his money into my bank account to make sure that I would be financially set if something were to happen. How he was talking, one would think something was going to happen soon.

Yet, weeks went by and no one heard anything from Smooth. Soon those weeks turned into two months. It is now August and I still can't grasp the fact the man who made me so happy is now missing. Tomorrow is our five year anniversary and sad thing is that I haven't talked to him at all. He has no longer called, texted, instant messaged me, Facebook chatted me, Skyped me... Nothing at all.

I feel that part of me is missing since he has been gone. My usual routine is not going the way it used to be. Just when I was getting use to him being in my life, now I have to turn around and get to use to him not being here. That isn't fair, but then again, life isn't fair.

If he was playing me, that is fucked up. How could you spend every single moment communicating with a person and make all these plans, get their hopes up, get engaged and even go half on a baby with a person, and then turn around and leave them high and dry?

That doesn't make sense. Yet for a situation like this, I truly don't know what to believe and what to think? Maybe he is playing me, or maybe something happened to him? I just pray that he is alive and not in jail. Then again, I just hope he gets back in contact with me if he is ok.

If I don't get in contact with him tomorrow on our special day, then I will just push these feelings aside and act as if this whole Sweetz and Smooth thing never happened. Which is sad, yet it is life. I'm really hurt, and if I don't hear from him tomorrow I will heartbroken. But aye, what doesn't kill me only makes me stronger. So I will just have to keep it moving and just hope he comes back to me.

Things were just moving so fast to me and it felt as though everyday was a constant change. Krazy and Kris were no longer together, I'm engaged and pregnant, and the Hot Boyz was changing drastically. The Hot Boyz was no longer hot on these streets. Some other gang was taking over, and Smooth wasn't here to change that. Just from that fact alone, I got worried about Smooth being dead or alive.

As I laid here in my bed of sorrow, dwelling on the new reality I'm facing, my cell phone began to ring. "Hello." I answered unenthused. "Hey girly, you ok?" The voice of Krazy traveled over the phone. "No…Still thinking about Smooth." I sighed. "Girl, I understand. I'm still trying to cope without Kris being in my world. But he ain't making it easy for me. How about we go out for lunch and have a little girl talk." She suggested. "Ok we can do that." I agreed. "Good, I will be over at your place in thirty ok?" "Ok." I replied, before hanging up.

Mariah Carey's "Side Effects" blasted throughout my loft as I hopped in my shower and began going through my daily routine. I wasn't in the dressy mood, so I slipped into my baby blue Juicy Couture jogging outfit, placed my feet into my silver and baby blue sandals, and pulled my wavy hair up into a high bun. While I was adding the finishing touches by placing my sunglasses and lip gloss on, Krazy busted into my loft.

"Bitch what are you doing busting up into my place like that?" I yelled playfully. "I guess you forgot I got an extra key huh?" She laughed, while flopping on my couch. "I know yo' ass got a key...But you still could've knocked first." I snapped. "Yeah ok...Like you were really doing something that I would be scared to walk in on." She sarcastically replied.

"You never know, I might've been getting my freak on!" I joked and stuck my tongue out at her. "Psssh...Yeah right, if I'm not getting none I know your ass for damn sure ain't getting none." Krazy retorted while rolling her eyes.

"Ugh...Whateva trick!" I laughed, while throwing a pillow at her. "Mmmhmm...You know I'm right." She laughed. "Whateva', So where are we going missy?" I asked while grabbing my Gucci bag off the kitchen counter. "I'm really feening some Buffalo Wild Wings right now." Krazy stated, while rubbing her stomach. "Aiight then let's go." I said while heading to the door. "Ok." Krazy agreed while jumping off the couch and following my lead.

"So how are you coping with this?" Krazy asked, while sipping on her pink lemonade at Buffalo Wild Wings. "I really haven't coped with it yet." I sighed. "I'm just confused on this, like why would he leave me high and dry like that? Smooth of all people know how I feel about people abandoning me. So for him to do that, that shit hurts like hell." I explained in pure sadness.

"Hell yeah. When that nigga comes back, I'm going to beat his ass for you my damn self. How are you going to leave my girl like that after you purposed to her and even got her pregnant? Like what the hell? He deserves an ass whooping!" Krazy exaggerated, causing me to laugh, something I haven't done in a while.

"That ole' tired ass yella' nigga...He ain't shit! He thinks he all pretty and shit...Bitchassness I swear!" She continued. "Girl, you are crazy." I laughed. "But you know I'm being real Sweetz, you are too good of a person to be getting treated like that." "Yeah, you right...I just don't know what to think when it comes to this situation. You know?" I replied, before I started tearing my chicken up. "Yeah...Since Kris and I broke up, he's just made things harder for me. You know that negro still call and text me every day?" She exclaimed.

"Say what?" I squealed in amazement. "Yeah girl, that fool is bi-polar, one minute he is cool, and the next minute he is cussing me out and calling me all kinds of names." Krazy finished. "Girl, he needs some help. I don't know why guys act so bitchmade these days." I said, thinking about all the losers my girls told me about who done them wrong.

"Hell yeah... I'm just tired of this shit. I see Kris all the time at the random places, people keep asking me about us and just everything reminds me of him. I need a change. I need to get the fuck out of here. I just might go to Cali." Krazy sighed. "Mmm... I might be right there with you girl. If Smooth doesn't contact me tomorrow on our anniversary, then I'm done with this shit. Being here is not going to do anything for me. All this gang shit, all these hating ass females, being known as a girlfriend or ex-girlfriend of a Hot Boy, I mean it's not doing anything good for us at all. It was fun when we was younger, but shit I'm about to be twenty and a mother at that. Partying and acting a fool is done for me, I have to grow up. I need to make a new move in my life and start of fresh. Not only for me, but for my baby." I explained.

"I feel the same way. I loved being with a Hot Boy, but like you said, we need to grow up and make changes." Krazy concurred.

"Yep...So I guess Cali it is. We should leave tomorrow night." I suggested. "Hell yeah...As always it's you and me against the world." Krazy said with a smile. "Of course, you're my ride or die bitch. Even when everyone else turns their back on us, we are all we got." I replied. "Aww I'm about to cry..." Krazy joked. "Whateva' trick! You ready to go?" I asked while getting out of the booth. "Yeah...Shit you never know, we just might run into Kris's crazy ass. Walk outside and bam there he is standing there." Krazy said, causing me to laugh. "Girl, you never know in this day and age." I agreed.

After paying for our food, we hopped in the car and headed back to my house to relax. Since this was our last night in Michigan we wanted to end it the right way...Drama free.

Kris:

Lil Wayne's "Brand New" blasted throughout the club, while I sat in the V.I.P section sipping on some Hennessey. The club was packed, females were all over the place looking right, and most importantly tonight was the night the H-Block gang would be in the building. I scanned all over the club only to see Samya. Our eyes locked as she walked towards my direction. Dressed in a sexy black dress that hugged her curves right, Samya headed up the stairs while her long curly weave flowed behind her.

"Hey Kris." She greeted. "Wassup Mya?" I said while licking my lips. I knew I had an effect on her, because she instantly bit her bottom lip from the excitement I caused her. She sat next to me and placed her hand on my knee.

"I did what you asked of me baby." She said with a smile. "Good job ma' " I replied, while staring into her eyes. Samya looked in my eyes for two seconds and quickly looked down. I knew she was a weak link because she couldn't even look me in my eyes long enough. Any female who can't look me in the eye is weak, and is not the woman for me. The only reason why I'm fucking with this girl is due to the fact that she was the sister of the head of the H-Block gang. The only way I could get close to them, was through her.

Before I knew it, the H-Block gang walked into the club dressed in all black. The whole club went crazy, like they were celebrities. I instantly thought about how the Hot Boyz used to make the clubs go crazy back in our prime. When that was me, I never thought the Hot Boyz would end, since in my eyes we were untouchable. Now look at how things have changed.

People never realize how quick good things can get snatched right from under you. One minute you're living it up, and the next minute it's taken away. The fame, the glory, the power... All that can be taken away in one hot second due to the choices that you may have made, or that someone else made. From that notion, I knew I had to stay on top of shit and make moves.

"J-Ro." Samya yelled out to one of the members. The male, who must have been J-ro, looked up at Samya, flashed a smile, and headed up to the V.I.P. After she introduced me to the H-Block gang, we began talking about the petty shit first and then we began talking business.

Things were going as planned, I was officially going to be a part of the H-Block gang and soon I was going to take over. I was going to not only take over the H-Block gang, but I was going to take over these streets. Since the Hot Boyz was no longer hot, Smooth was missing, and shit was just falling apart, I had to make moves. As the saying always go, drastic times cause for drastic measures.

CHAPTER 3: A FRESH START

__Krazy:__

"We're in California baby!" Sweetz squealed, in pure excitement as we walked down the beach trying to find a place to lie down and relax. "Hell yeah. We are finally away from all that craziness." I sighed of relief. "No Kris, no Smooth, no..." "Heyyyy Girls!" The annoying voice of Cashmere quickly cut me off, ruining my positive mood. That bitch always knew how to ruin a fucking day.

Sporting a Neon orange bikini that made her chocolate skin glow, Cashmere walked over to us while her wavy, black and purple extensions flowed behind her.

"What's up girls?" She gleamed. "Hey." Sweetz and I both replied dryly. "How are you enjoying Cali?" Cash interrogated, while we all began to lie out in our new founded location. "We wouldn't know. We just got here." I snapped. "Oh really?" She asked dumbfounded. "Yeah, we just got here like three hours ago. Moved our stuff in our condo, got our cars, and we went straight to the beach" Sweetz explained in a lighthearted manner, covering the bitterness I just spewed at Cashmere. "Oh that's cool...Well I could give you a tour of the city if you would like..." Cash suggested. "Sure, that would be nice." Sweetz quickly responded, knowing good and well I didn't want to be around that heffa'.

"Ooo, and you guys have to meet my man and his friends. They are the flyest things in Cali. Everybody who is somebody knows them." Cashmere boasted.

"Oh really...They're in a gang or something?" Sweetz inquired, asking the same thing I was thinking. "No...Why would you think that?" Cashmere scoffed. "Uhhh duh! Common sense says that if everybody knows them, they have to be hot, doing something on these streets." Sweetz said sarcastically, once again taking the words right out of my mouth. I loved that girl! We were so much alike, it's scary.

"What? No! My man is definitely not a gang banger; he is a businessman turning the real estate game out. He and his brother run Cali and he doesn't even have to gang bang to do it. He's not a coward like some." Cashmere said while flipping her hair, and sticking her nose up in the air, but also flipping this conversation to a heated debate. How the fuck is this chick going to try and act brand new on us? Like she is all uppity and would never fuck with a gangsta'...Wow!

"So you think gang members are cowards now?" Sweetz started. "Well, I'm just saying..." Cash began. "Hell no, Kris and

Smooth was never some damn cowards. Yo' ass just fucked with those whack ass wanna-be pimps and never had a real ass man." I flipped.

"You wish you could have a gang leader like one of them just so yo' ass can get a taste of what being real feels like." I continued. "Is that what you think huh?" She smirked. "And what the fuck does that mean?" I snapped. "What do you think it mean?" She sparked back. My temper began to flare and I knew it was a matter of time before I was going to whoop that ass. She deserved an ass whooping a long time ago, and I was ready and willing to give it to her fake ass.

"Look, I understand your man is a businessman and all that, but what you fail to realize is that that running and being in a gang weighs just as much a running and being in a business. They are the same thing. As far as I'm concerned, a businessman is a fucking coward because they would never be able to handle the shit that my baby Smooth and Kris been through...They wouldn't be able to last five fuckin' seconds." Sweetz began.

"So before you go bragging and boasting, and trying to put gang members down, you might want to do your fuckin' research and get your facts straightened out. Because right now you are surely not credible." Sweetz said, shutting this dumb ass conversation down. Cashmere should have known not to start shit she couldn't handle. If it wasn't for Sweetz, Cashmere would be getting sent to the hospital today, recuperating from a serious ass whooping.

"I'm sorry if I made you guys mad." Cashmere apologized. "Hmm!" I interjected sourly. "Yeah, well let's just stop talking and start relaxing." Sweetz suggested, while sipping on her virgin strawberry daiquiri. "Shit, I thought you would never ask. Hand me a drink Sweetz." I smiled.

"Well, ok. I thought we would continue having girl talk, but I guess we can hold it off 'til later huh?" Cashmere spoke nervously. "You damn right!" Sweetz and I agreed in unison. Not another word was spoken, while we continued to sip on our cool drinks and enjoy looking at the eye candy scattered all over the beach.

Spending a day with Cashmere was nothing short of exhausting, better yet annoying! Bad enough that the chick loves to talk until your ears bleed, but for her to boast brag about little things in her life was even worse. As soon as we entered the new condo Sweetz and I shared, I kicked my shoes off, and enjoyed the silence.

"I swear I never want to see Cashmere again! Why can't she just poof and disappear?" Sweetz complained. "You were the one who agreed to go on that tour with the bitch. You know I don't like her ass." I replied, while fixing a glass of orange juice from our kitchen.

"Yeah, but I wanted to know my way around Cali at least. Shit we can't come here not knowing where the mall is!" She exclaimed. "You right!" I laughed, while plopping on the couch next to her. "I was thinking today..." I started in between sips of my orange juice. "Mmmhmm..." Sweetz chimed in.

"Since we moved out of Michigan to start a new life, I want to do something different with my appearance. If I'm going to start off fresh, I want to make sure ya' girl is looking fresh as well." "Oh really? So what are you going to do?" Sweetz posed. "To switch my look up, I'm going to get my hair cut and get my eyebrow pierced." I said proudly.

"Ooo…That's a big step girly, you were the one who never wanted to cut your hair." Sweetz commented. "No, Kris never wanted me to cut my hair. But fuck him, I'm doing me now" I sparked. "I feel that girl. It's only six O'clock, you got nothing but time to do what you have to do." Sweetz said, hinting for me to make this move today.

"Yeah, why not do it today?" I expressed. "Shit, there is nothing stopping you missy." Sweetz smiled. "Aiight lets go" I jumped off the couch, grabbed my purse and headed out the door with Sweetz following my lead.

Before I know it, my ass was at the closest beauty salon getting my hair cut. I was tired of being Krazy, the cute plain girl rockin' a layered wrap, looking like all the rest of the chicks from back home. I was tired of being Krazy, the girlfriend of Hot Boy Kris, living my life through and for him. I was tired of feeling unfulfilled. When I came home that night I was liberated. I felt like a whole new woman. My jet black hair was now styled in a fly ass bob, complimented with swooped bangs dyed razzlin' red, and I now had a sexy ass eyebrow piercing.

Shit, how sexy I was looking and feeling, nobody could tell me nothing. This time I'm going to do things differently. I'm no longer Krazy, from this point forward I will now be known as Simone. There were definitely going to be changes made in my life and this was definitely a fresh start.

<u>Sweetz</u>

"Damn ma', why don't you give me a chance?" Asked the sixteen year old boy, from behind the counter of the coffee shop. It's been two weeks since we just moved to California and all these guys are coming at me way too strong. "For last time sweetheart, you are too young for me." I smiled. "But ma'...I can change your life." He boasted. All I could do to that remark was roll my eyes, and laugh at his ignorance. How in the fuck could a sixteen year old boy change my life if he couldn't even get into a club? I quickly grabbed my iced mocha latte, and headed to a booth outside where "Simone" was sitting.

"If another little boy, grown man, or old ass man come at me one more time...I'm going to start barking at his ass." I exaggerated while I sat down at the booth. "Girl you are crazy." Simone laughed. "I'm foreal, that little boy who is sixteen, tried to tell me that he could change my life... Wow I swear males these days are getting too bold." I explained in annoyance.

"You right...I'm not even stunting these dudes. I'm doing me right now." Simone chipped in. "Shit after what Smooth did to me, guys are the last thing on my list. I'm focused on bettering myself and creating a perfect environment for my baby. As far as I'm concerned I'm dating my own damn self! I mean let's be real here, who can do me better than myself? I will never lie, cheat, and for damn sure won't do myself wrong like these wack ass boys, who claim that they are a man." I lectured. "Girl I know that is right. Amen to that!" Simone laughed. Although she was laughing, I was dead serious. I'm not even thinking about any of the male species. My focus is my baby and I. This was a fresh start at a new life. No more Smooth, no more drama, no more lies. It is time to do things for me and only me.

"Girl you know that guys aren't going to get you nowhere except for getting fucked in the end." Simone snapped, breaking my thoughts. "You ain't never lied. But anywho' I'm not feeling this whole condo thing." I said, quickly changing the subject. "Hell yeah, I think we need to get a..." Simone started but was quickly interrupted by sexy deep male voice, "A House perhaps..."

Simone

I quickly turned around to see who the fuck this bitch was who cut me off. At one glance my pussy became instantly wet. This man could put Morris Chestnut to fucking shame. Standing at 6'5, with smooth deep chocolaty skin, and naturally short curly hair...Not the texturizer shit! This man was something out of my dreams. His almond shaped eyes were pitch black, his black nicely trimmed mustache was sexy as hell and his bright Colgate smile was breathtaking.

He was dressed professionally in a black suit and red tie to draw attention to his sexy ass. I don't know why, but it was just something about him was just so exotic. He looked as if he came from island descent. All I could do was stare at him in pure awe.

"I'm sorry for interjecting ladies, but I couldn't help but overhear your conversation about not enjoying your condo. I'm a real estate agent and I had to come to you guys and give you an offer you couldn't refuse" He explained. "Oh really?" I smiled. "Oh yes." He responded in the sexiest voice I ever heard. Damn, the things I would do to this man.

"Ok mister...All this talking about an offer we can't refuse, how about you offer us your name?" Sweetz said sarcastically. "Oh I'm sorry missy...My name is Jake." He smiled. "Jake huh? Well have a seat." I smirked. "My pleasure." Jake sat down at our table and stared intensely in my eyes.

Damn this man is just too much for me. "So tell me more about this offer." Sweetz urged in excitement. You could tell she was excited about getting a house, but I was excited about getting this man in my bedroom, and better yet playing the role of my man.

While Jake talked about real estate, I feigned to listen intensely, yet my mind wondered off to Mr. Jake and I making babies on the beach, rolling all in the sand, getting straight dirty! I couldn't help but to imagine those soft and sexy lips, that were now talking about houses, to be placed all over my body. By how wet I was getting just from looking at him, I would need to change my panties twice. I could just feel those big manly hands on me right now; one placed over my treasure, finger stroking my clit, and the other on my breast tracing circles on my nipples.

Damnit Simone! Calm your nerves girl....He is focused on his business, he isn't trying to be my one and only. So why am I so enwrapped with this man? I quickly grabbed my drink off the table, and began to take a sip to help calm me down. I couldn't help but feel eyes on me, so I looked up and as soon as his eyes locked with mine, butterflies fluttered in my stomach. I quickly lost focus on my concentration, and began choking on my water. "Girl are you ok?" Sweetz asked, while patting me on my back. "Yeah, yeah...I'm fine." I said in a rush, trying to catch my breath and recover from this embarrassing moment.

"I guess it got real good to you huh?" Jake chuckled. "Yeah, I guess." I said, chuckling it off, but all the while thinking, "if you only knew." "Well ladies, I have a closing that I have to make my way to, so here is my business card, and call me if you need anything." Jake enlightened while standing over us. "Anything huh?" I said while biting my bottom lip, and staring into his eyes. That is one thing about me, I love to stare directly in a man's eye. It lets me know just what type of person I'm dealing with.

"Yes...Anything. You know, I got La' nay's name, but I never caught your name..." "That's because I never threw it." I snapped. "Ooooh." Jake laughed. "You got me good ma'. But I like that...A little feistiness to you huh?" He continued. "It's more where that came from." I replied. "Well wouldn't I like to find out." Jake rejoined, once again in that sexy deep voice, causing my pussy to quiver. "My name is Simone by the way." "Simone huh? How about you give me a call later on this week and then we can set up a viewing of the house Simone." Jake suggested.

"I will make sure I do that." I smiled. "I'll be waiting...Well nice meeting you ladies, I'm sure I will be see you again." Jake said before parting, leaving me hot and wet.

"Girrrrlll...Are you ok?" Sweetz asked, looking at me like I had five heads. "No...That man right there just does something to me" I sighed in relief. "I can see that..." Sweetz laughed, shaking her head. "Was it that obvious?" I asked with a shocked face expression. "Girl, you looked like you was about to have an orgasm right in that chair" "Shit I really was" I said, causing both of us to laugh in unison. "I'm not going to lie, that was a fine ass chocolate man." Sweetz admitted.

"Fine is a fucking understatement when it comes to that man...I never had someone just make me feel like that, but all I know is... If he play his cards right, then he can definitely get some of this." I explained, while thinking about all the ways he could get a piece of me.

After our little girl talk, Sweetz and I made our way back to our condo and went our separate ways to our bedroom. As I laid in my bed, with De'angelo from Making the Band Four singing "Journey" in my background, thoughts of Jake traveled through my mind. I couldn't get my mind off him. That night I made myself cum all to the vision of Jake and I having rough sex in my head. That was when I knew that it was something about this man that had me hooked.

Sweetz

This pregnancy shit is no joke. I'm only two months pregnant and I'm an emotional mess. I'm always exhausted and I eat like I'm a three hundred pound woman. If I ever see Smooth out on these streets, I'm going to beat that Negro with my shoe until the white meat shows! Getting me pregnant, having me gain weight, and turning into a queen bitch, all because he wanted a baby!

"Hell no!"...That's what my ass should've said when he offered that proposition. But did I? No...I agreed upon this because I loved his ass. I swear love is for the fuckin' birds. Thoughts of how I was going to beat Smooth's ass if I ever seen him clouded my head, as I sat on the couch eating my sugar cookies.

"Look at yo' fat ass..." I quickly turned around only to see Simone dressed in a white buttoned up blouse, accented by a red cardigan, a black pencil skirt, and the matching black Christian Louboutin pumps with the red on the bottom.

"Bitch don't come at me like that. And where are you going looking all cute?" I snapped. "To work!" Simone giddily replied while grabbing her black bag off the counter. "Ooo, well go and do your thing then." "You know I will. Some people aren't as financially set like others who can sit on the couch and be lazy all day." Simone jabbed. "Don't hate heffa', I'm a princess so I can do that." I said, proudly.

"Yeah princess my ass!" Simone scoffed. "Haters these days...Gosh!" I said playing innocently. "Yeah whatever trick. No one is hating on your spoiled ass." Simone remarked.

"Anyway, I called Mr. Jake last night." Simone smiled as she changed the subject. "Ooo did you now?" "Yep, I have a viewing with him tomorrow." She gleamed. "Ooo you betta' go get that man!" "You know I will! Now let me go and make this money." Simone said with assurance, before leaving me all alone in the condo.

<u>Simone</u>

As I walked into Lattermoore & Lattermoore Legal Services, I was greeted by a vanilla faced, blue eyed, blonde with "Stacey" printed on her nametag. "Hello Ms. Simmons, welcome to our facility." "Well thank you." I replied, while following her upstairs.

After getting the "New Employee" tour, Stacey began to show me how to work the printing and copying machines, when a sexy male voice interrupted our tutorial. "Now come on Stacey, you know this beautiful lady is smart enough to work a copy machine. Isn't that right beautiful?"

I quickly turned around to see a new eye candy in this office. He stood at a mere 5'9", with smooth peanut butter brown skin, round dark brown eyes and a sexy shiny bald head. "Of course." I smiled righteously.

"Mmm...I like that attitude Simone." He smiled back, while looking at not only my name tag, but my figure as well. Such a man! "Well thank you mister..." "Mr. Lyles. Torrian Lyles." He interjected. "Well Stacey, you did a great job hiring my new secretary. I will let you keep training this beautiful lady while I go to this meeting with Mr. Lattermoore." He explained before parting his way, and leaving me in shock. So my new boss is Mr. Torrian Lyles? Wow, this will be an interesting job.

"So what do you think about him?" Stacey interrogated, quickly interrupted my thoughts. "I mean what can I think?" I laughed. "I just met him." "Hmmm…Since you're the new girl, I will inform you on some things." Stacey started, leaning in closer to me. The look on her face was so devious, and proved my assumptions right. I knew that she was one who couldn't be trusted.

"Torrian is a flirt. Matter of fact, he is the biggest flirt in the office. But everyone knows, when you want a raise, he is the one you can guarantee to get it from. His uncles are Mr. Ken and Daniel Lattermoore, making Torrian the next top authority under them. Just give him what he wants, and your days here will be worthwhile, and your checks will be bigger than you can imagine." She whispered.

"Oh really now?" I posed. "Mmmhmm!" She said, while grinning like a Cheshire cat. "So how big is your check, being the secretary and personal assistant of Mr. Lattermoore?" I asked out of curiosity. "Over 120 thousand." She smiled, leaving me in shock.

Damn! The average salary for an legal secretary was around $54,000. If this chick can make over a $120,000, then I know I can definitely hit the jackpot if I fucked with the right one, and that right one was Mr. Lyles....Torrian Lyles to be exact!

CHAPTER 4: DECEIVING ACTS

<u>Simone</u>

After of hours of working on my first day at Lattermoore & Lattermoore, Mr. Lyles asked me to go to lunch with him. My first mission accomplished! All I had to do was get him attracted to my physical, intrigued by mysterious personality, and he would soon be in the palm of my hand. As we sat inside The Palm in downtown Los Angeles, I couldn't help but notice how sweet this man really was.

"So tell me about you Simone." Mr. Lyles suggested with pure excitement in his eyes. "I'm not that interesting." I giggled before sipping on my drink. "What? That is a lie. You know you live a hell of a life!" He exclaimed. "Maybe I do." I smirked. "Or maybe I don't...Shit, my life has been hell for years, so I definitely don't have a hell of a wonderful life." I continued, being real with him. "Aww...How could your life be hell at a mere nineteen?" He scoffed.

"Trust me, if I told you, you would never believe me. I've been through shit that your mind couldn't even grasp." I replied defiantly. "Oh really?" "Yes...You couldn't handle five minutes in my shoes." I finished. "But you're not telling me anything about your life." Torrian said, looking at me with sincere eyes.

"Why should I? My past is not my present, and definitely won't be an indicator of my future. So why should I waste my time, and my breath talking about it. Detroit is nothing like L.A and the people there are not even a quarter as pleasant and not to mention superficial as the people here. It's not so much about status there... It's a real dog eat dog world. And I'll be damned if my ass get ate." I poured out, giving Mr. Lyles a taste of how "Krazy" use to think.

"Wow..." He started. "Just...Damn...I see." He uneasily replied due to my seriousness. "So anyway, are you single Simone?" He asked, changing subjects. "I sure am Mr. Lyles." I smiled, while leaning back in my chair. "You can call me Torrian...I feel so old when you call me Mr. Lyles outside of work." He smiled. "Ok Torrian, and how old are you?" I inquired flirtatiously. "Thirty-one my dear." Torrian quickly responded. "Ooo...Getting old aren't we there?" I joked. "Aww shut up!" He laughed.

"Mmmhmm...So where is the old lady hiding at? You know your wife?" I said sarcastically. "I don't know, because I don't have one." He said sadly. "Aww, why not?" I asked, lightly placing my hand on his arm. "I walked in on my ex-girlfriend cheating on me with this white guy. In my house, in my bed." He explained broken down. Although it was sad, that shit is nothing compared to what I been through. I tried to be sentimental, but the Krazy in me would not let that happen.

"Pssh! Negro please! That shit is nothing compared to what I been through . Shit, if she wanted some vanilla in her chocolate then fuck her! You kicked her ass out like you were supposed to, now it's time for you to move on, and forget it ever happened. You are attractive, successful and got money out the ass...Shit you can fuckin' buy a new bitch if you wanted to!" I began, causing Torrian to fill the room of laughter.

"Foreal. You could buy you whatever kind of female you would like. And if she fucks up, you can get another one. Do you know who you are? Shit. You better tell 'em like this, ' if you fuck up on me I will buy a new you!' Watch their ass straighten their act up real quick." I ranted.

"Man, I wish that shit was the only little petty drama of my life. I would be happy with that. I would chuck up my deuces and move on... Happy as I want to be. So my words to you, is to not sweat it. You shouldn't have to worry about a female at all honey, just make your money and do you." I continued, telling him like it is.

"Man, you are so blunt and real. I love it." Torrian said, trying to catch his breath from laughing so hard. I was dead serious, but I guess to him it was too funny. "I mean hey, I'm just telling you how it is and how it should be for ya'." I shrugged.

"Yeah...I really like you Simone. You are a realist and I like that in you. Something you don't see in women lately. I think we will become really good friends outside of work. Don't you agree?" Torrian asked, while placing his hand on top of mine. "Oh yes." I looked him directly in his eyes and saw pure lustful desire. He wanted me, and I wanted more money. Two corrupted motives, but I knew it would be one powerful outcome.

I knew that this was the only way I could get ahead of the game, and he would make it very easy for me. Yet there was a feeling in the pit of my stomach, telling me that something wasn't right about this. Shit, oh well! I was on a mission and I was going to do anything to get it accomplished, by any means necessary.

Sweetz

"Wait, isn't she pregnant? Why is she here?" "Why is there a pregnant girl in our class?" "Hmmm...Someone got knocked up..." These were all the comments I heard as I walked into my Philosophy class taught at UCLA. I swear people are so damn ignorant. Just because I'm pregnant does not mean that I can't go to school, and receive the proper education that I deserve. Shit, little do they know, I'm smarter and richer than all of these ignorant fools. I continued to keep my head up high as I sat in my seat and waited for the professor to come and teach this class.

After five minutes of hearing people snickering about me being the infamous pregnant girl in class, my professor walked in. He stood tall and firm at 6'4" with smooth golden brown skin, shiny, thick black locks of curls, with a sexy mustache and goatee reminding me of Jon B. His hazel, almond shaped eyes were captivating, and the way he dressed was appeasing to the eye.

There was just something about him that sparked an instant attraction. One look at him and I instantly got moist. Thoughts of him being my lover played throughout my head until reality hit me. First, he is my professor, and second, I'm pregnant by Smooth. So the chance of this man and I ever becoming an item, was slim to none.

"Good morning class." The deep sexy voice traveled throughout the room, interrupting my thoughts. "My name is Mr. Shamir...But you guys can call me Jayden. I'm only thirty-five, so

I'm not that old." He laughed, showing off his perfect set of pearly whites and a deep set of dimples. "You really don't look thirty-five at all Jayden," said a woman from the back of the room, trying to flirt. "Well thank you, Ms..." He paused. "Calapri, it's a Brazilian name." She interjected.

Getting annoyed, I quickly turned around to see this bitch. My eyes laid upon a golden tanned woman, about the age of twenty-five, with long black hair, and chocolate brown eyes. The way she was smiling so hard, made it obvious that she wanted to sleep with him. I felt myself quickly getting disgusted, so I turned back around and faced Jayden with an unpleasant face expression. If there is one thing I hate in this world, it is thirsty females. I truly had my share of them preying on my man, back when I was dating Smooth.

Seeing the expression in my face, Jayden stood there and stared at me with a smile. "Is there something wrong miss?" He asked. "No, I'm just annoyed about some things." I responded. "Aww you are too beautiful to be annoyed, and to be carrying a new life, there is surely no reason to be annoyed." He said, while staring me directly in the eye. "Life is something important. Life is something to be cherished. It's a gift. It proves our existence and should never should be taken for granted. With that in mind, let's get into chapter one." He explained while walking around the room.

Throughout the class, Jayden continuously locked eyes with me. It was something about the way he looked at me that was so intense, as if he could see right through me. Every time I looked into his eyes, I gained a deeper feeling for this man. The warm feeling of being safe and protected, almost close to feeling loved.

"Ok class, my time is up. We will continue on Thursday." Jayden ended, standing tall in front of the class. Students quickly rushed out of the classroom, eager to do their various tasks for the day. Yet I was taking my sweet time to gather my belongings, on purpose of course.

"So what is your name?" Jayden inquired. "La'nay." I replied, while turning around and staring into his hazel eyes. "Nice, I see that you were really into my topic today in class. It is something in your eyes that has this twinkle and passion in it." He explained while sitting on his desk. "Well thanks, I guess." I laughed. "I know corny right." He chuckled, while looking down shyly. "No, it's actually very sweet." I smiled.

"You are just so beautiful." He said softly. "I know you are my student, but you are so exotic looking. What is your ethnicity?" He asked. "I'm Nigerian and Native American." "Ahhh nice. I'm Trinidadian. So we are kinda' close." He replied, causing me to laugh. "I guess...If you say so mister." "Oh you don't think so?" He smiled. "Hell no! Nigeria and Trinidad are two different places, two different worlds." I explained.

"Mmmhmm, so where are you from?" He asked staring into my eyes and licking his lips, turning me on even more. "Detroit, but I just moved here not even a month ago." "Ohhh Detroit eh? Home of the...The Mighty Lions." He said sarcastically. "Boo! Please don't embarrass me." I scoffed, causing us both to laugh in unison. Since we both knew that the Lions were not that mighty in Detroit. "Ok, ok. I won't do you like that! But that is interesting. What made you move here?" Jayden asked, changing the subject.

"I needed a change, a new lifestyle you know? So me and my girl packed up our shit and moved here." "Yeah, but how does the father of your child feel about that?" Jayden posed, making this conversation uncomfortable for me. Sensing the change in my whole manner, Jayden tried to explain further.

"I mean, to have such a beautiful and dainty woman to carry your child, that is a privilege and he should be honored so why would he let you just leave. I mean I would have to put my foot down and tell you no. No mother of the child of mine is leaving without me. You know?" He chuckled. "Yeah, well if he was actually around when I needed him, then I would still be there with him. But he is M.I.A as of now. I don't know where he is." I sighed. "Damn, I don't want to get all in your business. But it seems like you have a hell of a story to tell, excuse my French since I'm a teacher and all." Jayden replied in a serious manner. "It's fine, and your right I do have a story to tell. Maybe one day I will share it with you." I said, while grabbing my belongings and getting ready to head off. Before I could walk away, Jayden gently grabbed my hand, and stared into my eyes for a minute of silence.

"Look, I want you to know that outside of the classroom, I 'am here for you. Whenever you get lonely, sad, and just need someone... I 'am here. You have my number. Just call me." He explained sincerely. I don't know why, but this one sentence touched me deeply.

Since I been here, I've been feeling so down and out. So lonely, like something is missing. It feels like it's just me against the world. Now here is this man, who doesn't know me from Adam, and he said the words I've been waiting to hear for so long. Yet to trust another man is the hardest thing to do after you've been hurt so bad. It is just something to think about.

"Ok...I will keep that in mind Jayden." I said softly, before walking away. I couldn't believe that I'm feeling this man so much, but he isn't just some man, he was my teacher! The crazy thing is, it has only been day one of class. I can only imagine how it's going to be throughout the semester.

<u>Simone</u>

Today was the day. I was going to view houses with the one and only Mr. Sexy a.k.a Jake. Since I haven't bought a new car yet, Jake was going to pick me up to show me the houses, and maybe show me a little bit more.

I was dressed to kill in my sexy royal purple, curve hugging, Versace dress and matching purple Christian Louboutin 6" pumps. My bob was looking fly as hell and my makeup was done to perfection, thanks to Sweetz. With my sexy Vickie Secrets underneath this dress, waiting to be seen, and my soft chocolate skin glowing due to my body shimmer, I had no doubt that my plan was going to be a success.

T-pains "I can't believe it" blasted throughout my room, letting me know that it was Jake calling. "Hello." I smiled. "Well Hello Ms. Simone, I'm right in front of your house. Would you like me to come in or would you like to just come out?" His sexy deep voice traveled into my ear. "I will just come out, no need for you to come out of your car and waste time. Since we have things to do you know?" I said in my sexy tone. "Ok." He chuckled. "The ball is in your court. So I'm going to sit here and wait." He said, ending our conversation. A huge smile planted across my face as I quickly sprayed on my Gucci perfume, checked my sexy ass out in the mirror to make sure everything was in place, and made my way out the door.

The sun was shining bright on this beautiful day. Yet the cool breeze flowed through my bob, as I gracefully walked towards

Jake's black 2008 Bugatti Veyron car. I never even heard of such a car until I got here, but I have to admit that bitch was fly. A fly car with Jake sitting in the driver's seat made it ooze with attraction. The Balla's and Street celebrities in Detroit didn't have shit on the real movers and shakers in L.A. You could tell that there was a huge difference of class and swag between these people. I could even see myself changing in this short amount of time of being here! Simone and Krazy are two different people I'm no longer a "Hot girl" on those streets making hits and being the ride or die for a man who was up to no good. Now I'm a white collared working woman, living in L.A and associating myself with high powered movers and shakers. Wow, Such a drastic change!

"Well hello there Ms. Simone." Jake greeted me, interrupting my thoughts as I entered his luxurious car. "Hello Mr. Jake." I smiled back and sat in the comfortable leather seat. "You look very beautiful today...Just had to let you know." He complimented, while staring at my attire with those enticing eyes.

"Mmm, well thank you...You look handsome yourself." I replied while staring back into his eyes. "Well you know I try." He said playfully, causing me to laugh. "I guess...So can we go now?" I interjected. "You are over here trying to be Mister Sauvé and we have business to handle. You're a businessman, I shouldn't have to tell you that." I said sarcastically. "Yeah, Yeah, Yeah...Lets go." He joked, before driving off to our first destination.

The whole ride was calm and pleasant. It was something about him that allowed me to unwind and be transparent with him. I could really be myself around him, no worries, and no false persona. With Kris, I could never do such a thing, I had to be that ride or die bitch, showing no remorse, and keeping all my emotions built in. The thought alone saddens me, and I never want to be like that again.

"You're going to love this house I picked out for you...You are going to go crazy when you see this." He smiled, showing off his one dimple. "Oh really?" I inquired. "Yes!" He exclaimed, full of excitement. I stared out the window, enjoying the beautiful scenery of these big and extravagant houses. Suddenly we were driving in an area that looked like the straight hood. What the fuck?

Turning on a street called Avalon Boulevard, Jake pulled up in front of this green and yellow house. It was a big group of guys across the street dressed in all black. Now, me being a hot girl, I'm not scared of no negro and no bitch! Although I might look like an uppity woman right now, I'm still that Krazy bitch!

"Why are we here Jake? I know your ass did not take me to the damn hood to show me a house." I said calmly. "Wow, you're not scared?" He asked in shocked. "Hell no...This is just like the eastside of Detroit to me. You must not know who you are dealing business with!" I said with full blown attitude. I can't believe this fool thought I was one of those scared females. He definitely got me mistaken!

"So why the fuck did you bring me here Jake?" I asked once again. No reply. "I'm not going to repeat my fucking self. Are you tryin' to set me up? Is this a fuckin' hit, cause if it is I will definitely kill a nigga first before my ass go down." I spewed out in pure anger. Krazy was now approaching. Damnit, I worked so hard not to let her come back. But shit, if this was how it's going down, my ass will put up a hell of a fight before I get taken out.

Getting ready to pull out my weapon from my purse, I was encountered with laughter. "What the fuck are you laughing at?" I interrogated with a raised eyebrow. "You." Jake said, while still rolling in laughter. "You think my ass would do some shit like that to you?" He asked. "I don't know what the fuck to think bitch." I spat, causing his happy disposition to change quickly.

"Wait, hold on Simone. I'm not a bitch, so you need to calm down with that rowdiness; I was just messing with you. This is my old neighborhood, and that house is my old house." Jake said in a grim tone. "Oh yeah?" I asked, not believing what he said. "Yes really." He replied defiantly. The look in his eye let me know he was genuine, and softened up my demeanor. "Ok...I guess I'm sorry. But you can't play around like that. You was about to get your ass beat foreal." I said calmly, finally letting my guard down again.

"I know you should've seen your ass. How you were talking, I would have thought you were one of those gangster girls." He laughed, but little did he know, I really was. I laughed along to play it off, but all the while I was thinking "If he only knew." Kris and I did hits like this all the time. He would get in good with the target, take them to an isolated destination, and then I would come and take them out nice and clean. So of course I would have my guard up when he brought me to this ugly ass green and yellow house.

"This is my old neighborhood. My mom was an immigrant from Trinidad, and she moved us here when I was four and when my big brother Jayden was eleven. Our father died before he could make it here because of his illness. So me and my big brother lived here in this hood. My brother had it rougher than me. Being the oldest he had to take care of home and protect my bad ass too. I was always trying to be like all the others out here on these streets, tryin' to be thug but he wasn't having that. He was a firm believer of education and success you know?" Jake began.

"I could never get with that school shit, but when I lost my best friend Marty to a drive-by, that was when shit changed. I stayed in school, graduated high school, went to college, and flipped this real estate game out. Got my momma out of this hell hole, and I 'am who I 'am today." Jake explained.

"Wow. I admire that a lot Jake," was all I could say after he gave me his spill. I knew this would be the best time for me to tell him about me, but then again why would I want to even discuss my past life? It's too soon to tell him my life story. He isn't my man; He really isn't even a friend... He is just Jake! So the thought of me telling him about me being the ex- girlfriend of a "Hot Boy" is not happening. "Well, let me show you the real house that you've been waiting on." Jake smiled, before pulling off and taking me to my real destination.

As we drove into the neighborhood, I instantly remembered Torrian telling me about Baldwin Hills and how everyone in the community was successful black men and women, who were so friendly, but of course I didn't believe him! Yet as soon as got out the car there was a black family next door, who instantly greeted us with a pleasant "Hello."

Back in Detroit, this would never take place. Saying hello to a stranger was like a severe felony. But hey, this is a new place, and a new lifestyle that I could definitely get use to.

As Jake showed me around this wonderful house, all I could do was stare in pure awe. This extravagant house in Baldwin Hills was nothing short of breathtaking. Three stories, six bedrooms, four bathrooms, island style kitchen and the best attribute was the window landscape wall facing the community from the common room.

I see these houses on MTV Cribs, but I never really seen one in person. Yeah, being a Hot Boyz's girlfriend, you would think that I would have been in a house like this, but there is a huge difference between blood money and clean money. I lived in fairly nice houses while being with Kris, and there was the Hot Boyz mansion. Yet none of which portrayed pure clean innocence.

This house exuded charisma, perfection, and pure elegance. No blood was shed to get this house, no drugs were sold to earn income to create and build this house... Instead this was clean, hard earned, money used to purchase this home and it would now be mine...The right way. Finally this will be something for me, and not Kris. Just this thought alone touched me deeply, man how I've came a long ass way.

"You like it?" Jake asked while we stood in the living room. "I love it." I replied, overwhelmed with the beauty of this house. I stood in front of the window landscape facing the suburban street and stared in pure awe. I was so enwrapped in my own little world that I forgot all about Jake.

As soon as I felt his warm breath crawling down the back of my neck, and his hands slowly wrapping around my waistline, chills instantly traveled up my spine. "Well it's all yours sexy." He whispered into my ear. I closed my eyes and softly exhaled. I wanted this man so damn bad. From the moment I first laid eyes on him, I knew that I wanted to jump his bones.

"Do you know how bad I want you Simone?" Jake asked, while slowly caressing my body through my dress. "How bad?" I said softly. "Too much for words." He replied lowly, while slowly unzipping my dress. "Well then show me." I said boldly, as my dress hit the ground.

I was now left with nothing on but my sexy purple and black lace bra and thong set that accented my thick, southern curves, and my purple pumps. I was still facing the window, letting the whole community see my sexy body that stood before the man I feigned for. He was my desire, he was the one who would satisfy my needs right here in front of this window and I didn't give a damn who would see us.

Jake aggressively grabbed me by my neck, pushed me into the window and ripped the thong and bra right off my body. I never felt so weak, so vulnerable, yet so damn turned on like I did now.

"Mmm, stick it out girl." He groaned. Just as he asked, I arched my back and allowed him to get a good look at my thick pussy from the back. "Damn, that pussy is so fat and wet... Just like I like it." He commented, before gently kissing me on the back of my neck. Even though that wasn't my spot, something about his lips made my pussy quiver as soon as his lips touched me. I couldn't help but let a moan down. My body began trembling from the good head this man was putting on me. Damn how could this shit be so good? Before I knew it, a huge orgasmic wave took over my body. With my hands imprinted on the window, my whole body shook and I squirted all over the place.

"Damn baby... You're a squirter too!" Jake said while standing back up from behind me. "Let me see if this dick can make that pussy squirt more than my tongue." He said in the sexiest voice, causing me to get wet again. Damn this man just does so much to me. After placing a condom on his soldier, Jake thrusted inside me, causing me to scream in pleasure. His dick was so damn thick, instantly hitting my g-spot... and he hasn't even started yet! I knew from then on, this sexcapade was going to be very interesting.

Before I knew it, Jake was pounding my pussy long and hard all while I was standing against the window with an arched back, letting the world see him fucking me. Tears of pleasure flowed down my face as he continued to manhandle this pussy. I squirted over and over, countless times! This sex was so intense, yet it was by far the best. I never been fucked like this, but I knew that this would definitely not be my last.

After three hours of sexing it up all over my new house, Jake and I laid on the living room carpet under a blanket that we found on the couch, and stared into each other's eyes. "Damn...That was so good." I smiled. "Hell yeah...I don't know if I'm ever going to let you go. I'll be damned if another man has you." Jake replied with a smirk. "Shut up! You're just sayin' that cause you got some of this goodness." I laughed.

"Naw, I'm serious girl. I really have strong feelings for you Simone. I want to be there for you, I want to play a role in your life. Not just as a friend or a lover...But as your man and soon to be husband." Jake said in a serious manner. All I could think was wow!

Jake

I continued to observe Simone after pouring out my emotions. It was something about her that touched my soul. I wanted to be with her, but there was only one thing that held me back.

After dropping Simone back off at her condo, I made my way back home in the black night. Only to be greeted with a "Where the fuck you been?" Dressed in a red silk housecoat, with her hair in curlers and some white, thick cream shit covered on her face, was the one and only Cashmere.

"Baby, I told you I was out handling business." I sighed while taking off my tie. "Hmm...Business my ass! I cooked you dinner and you didn't even show up until five hours later. I called and texted yo' black ass, and did I get a response? Hell no!" Cashmere ranted. I went to my room and continued to strip out of my clothes, as Cashmere trailed behind me. While she continued going on and on, it only went in one ear and out the other. I'm tired of coming home to her bitching every night. We've been together for four months. I've known her for a while, I thought she was a cutie with a nice ass booty, but something up in that head wasn't right. She was just off, I don't know what it is but she needs some professional help.

There would be days where she was just the sweetest thing, wouldn't even hurt a fly. Yet there would be days where she would just flip out and turn into a crazy ass woman. A whole different woman who would yell, scream, and throw shit.

I try to hang in there, but a man can only take so much. My time was almost up with her. "Jake I hate when you don't listen to me." She cried. "Look Cash, I'm tired. I work too damn hard to come home to you bitching every night. I've been patient baby, I really have. But I can only take so damn much dealing with your ass. You fuck around and trip on me again, I'm leavin' your ass. No ifs', ands', or buts' about it!" I commanded before rolling over and trying to take my black ass to sleep.

As a result of my ultimatum, Cashmere ran into the bathroom to cry her eyes out, but tonight I was not going to console her. It's no longer about her, so tonight I'm getting some sleep, and tomorrow I'm going to see Simone.

<u>Simone</u>

"Simone! I'm so glad to see you!" Stacey greeted happily, welcoming me with a huge hug. It was obvious that she was drunk on this Saturday night. Yet she wasn't the only one feeling good at this work party that Lattermoore & Lattermoore was hosting. "I'm glad to see you too Stacey." I laughed. "Girrrrrrl you look so good in that dress." She complimented after pulling away from the hug, and taking a good look at my attire. Looking good was an understatement on this night. Dressed in my curve hugging, black Roberto Cavalli cocktail dress that was adorned with a red waistband, my bob was now styled in a curly updo, and my feet were accented by my black and diamond studded Christian Louboutin 6" inch pumps. "Well thank you Stacey." I replied with a smile.

I scanned the room only to lock eyes with the infamous Torrian. Flashing me his sexy smile, Torrian excused himself from the group of men he was talking to, and headed over to my direction. "You look stunning tonight Ms. Simone." Torrian praised as he greeted me with a warm and inviting hug.

"You too Mr. Torrian." I flirted in response. "Do I really?" He joked. "Don't act stupid now...You better take my compliment and like it." I snapped playfully, causing him to chuckle. "Ok, ok...Geesh don't bite my head off." He continued. "Not yet." I winked and trailed off to the bar. Although I was still nineteen, the bartender was just giving away free drinks without asking age. He probably figured everyone here was twenty- one and up, yet why would I complain?

After five tequila shots with Stacey's crazy ass, and two long island iced teas, I was feeling really toasted. No wonder why she was so happy to see me. Lil Wayne ft. T-pains "Got Money" blasted throughout the hall causing everyone; black, white, and delights, to head to the dance floor and got crazy. Torrian quickly made his way behind me, placed his hands on my waist, and allowed me to twerk him like he never had it before.

Song after song and drink after drink, Torrian and I became closer than expected and the sexual tension was driving me crazy. I swear this liquor makes me so horny. Damn and Jake is out of town this weekend too. So who else would be a perfect sex toy candidate? Torrian of course!

The party was quickly approaching to an end, so Torrian and I sat at the bar ending the party off right with another drink. "How are you feeling Simone?" Torrian asked, staring me down seductively. "Mmm, mmm, mmm, Good!" I laughed. "Oh yeah?" He said in a sexy voice as he placed his hand on my knee. "Yeah..." I said softly, while I felt his hand move further up my thigh.

"You better stop..." I purred, as his hands moved further up in between my legs. The look in his eyes let me know that there was no way he was going to stop. Just the feeling of him touching me was turning me on, damnit Simone!

"Try to be discreet, we are out in public, in front of our co-workers." I whispered. Torrian laughed. "Ok, I will wait 'til later." He said as he moved his hand. "Who s-said there was going to be a laaaaaaaater." I slurred sarcastically. "It's like that huh?"

Torrian asked. "Yep!" I laughed as I hopped off the stool and grabbed my belongings. "We will see." He said lowly as he followed me out of the building. The cool wisp wind kissed my face as I stood outside and admired the stars shining up in the sky. It's funny how you are so busy and focused on various things, yet you never take the time out to appreciate and enjoy the simple things in life.

"So how are you getting home Simone?" Torrian inquired, interrupting my special moment. "I don't knooow..." I slurred once again, causing him to chuckle at my drunkenness. "Would you like me to drive?" "Yeah." I answered like an innocent child. "Ok." He replied, before gently grabbing my hand and taking me over to his car.

"So where are we going?" Torrian asked while buckling up his seat belt. "Hmm...I don't want to go to my place." I whined. "Well my place is getting remodeled, so how about we get a room?" He suggested, while strolling down the brightly lit street. "I don't care." I replied, while staring out the window. The alcohol continued to sink in each minute, causing me to gradually lose my vision, and my body to feel more in depth with the music playing in the car. "Ms Pretty Pussy" by Plies blasted throughout the car, making me get wetter and wetter by the time we arrived to the Hilton.

As I tried to step out the car, wooziness hit me hard and my legs felt paralyzed. "Torrian! I can't walk baby." I cried out. "Ok baby." Torrian replied, smiling hard at the fact that I called him baby. With a quickness, he made his way over to my side of the car and helped me walk into the hotel. I began to doze off as I sat and waited for him to check us in. Next thing I knew, we were both in a stopped elevator.

"W-What are you doing?" I stuttered. "You will see." He said, as he aggressively pent me up against the closest wall. Torrian began kissing me so aggressively and passionately, as if he's been waiting for this moment for a lifetime. While gently choking me with one hand, he fingered my pussy under my dress with the other hand. The way he was shoving his fingers in and out of my pussy in a fast paced motion, made me want to cum just from that alone.

"You are just so damn sexy Simone." He whispered into my ear, that he previously began licking and sucking on, causing me to shiver and moan. "You like that huh?" "Yesss!" I squealed as his thumb vibrated against my clit. I closed my eyes and enjoyed this pleasure he was giving me, until all of a sudden it stopped.

Torrian backed away from me and resumed the elevator. "Why did you stop?" I asked while breathing heavily. "I just wanted to warm you up before we get into the room." He said in a deep voice. I couldn't help but smile, this man was a freak. Who would've thought? As soon as we stepped into the hotel room, our clothes quickly hit the floor and it was on. Torrian was so aggressive, he almost put me in shock. Yet when I was on top riding the fuck out of that little eight inch dick, he couldn't even handle it. With my ass bouncing up and down, swallowing that dick up with my pussy, I leaned my head down to his ear and said "You can't handle this pussy if you tried. This is too much for you baby." "I can handle it." He said in between groans.

I laughed at him for even thinking that he could hang with me. All the dicks I fuck were at least ten inches or better. His little dick was not doing shit for me. He was just tickling the pussy. Just for kicks, I began bouncing harder and faster on that dick. "Slow doooown!" He pleaded.

"Hell no, you're going to take this pussy." I said as I continued to bounce harder and faster on that dick. Instantly, within minutes he screamed out like he was my bitch, and came faster than ever. I rolled off him, not even satisfied, and went to sleep. I will just wait for Jake to make me cum like I'm supposed to.

The next morning, I woke up, grabbed my stuff, and quickly crept out the hotel room while he was still sleep. If I had a conscious I would actually feel bad, but me still being Krazy, I could give two fucks about having sex with him to get to the top. Shit, you have to do what you have to do, all in order to make it in this world. So if I have to throw him some pussy every now and then to get a raise, and no longer depend on Kris and his money, then so be it.

Cashmere

"I'm tired of your shit Jake!" I screamed, while throwing a plate at the wall next to the front door. "What the fuck are about talking about?" He yelled while standing in the doorway, with a perplexed face expression. I couldn't take this shit. I was tired of always being the bitch on the side. Why are these guys so damn trifling? "I read the fucking text message on your phone. Yeah, leaving your cell phone here was a bad move Jake." I explained with my hands on my hip. "What?" He said in shock while walking inside the house. "Don't act like you don't know motherfucker! You're fucking Simone...Simone of all the damn bitches in the world Jake? You just had to fuck the bitch that was my friend." I screamed in anger. "She's your friend? Really now" He laughed.

"I never knew a crazy ass person like you could keep a friend. Shit can you even make one? Your ass is so damn scandalous. How dare you come in my house, cause all this damn commotion about me catching feelings and having relations with her, when you are screwing that cat from Detroit." He retorted, jabbing me below the belt.

"You know what Cashmere? I warned you the last time that if you trip on me again then I'm leaving your ass. I meant what I said from every bone in my body, so it's time for you to pack your shit and leave." He said calmly. "Leave? You want me to leave Jake? You are choosing this bitch over me?" I said in disbelief.

"D-Did I fucking stutter? Get your shit and get the fuck out. I will give you thirty minutes and if you don't have your shit together, I will throw the shit out myself. Don't worry about the keys I'm changing the locks. Just get the fuck out and leave me alone." He explained coldly. What the fuck? "Fuck you Jake. You want me to leave then I will leave." I screamed while heading upstairs to the room.

I gathered all my belongings while we continued exchanging foul words. With my suitcases in my hand, I stood in the doorway and mugged Jake one last time. "You got what you asked for Jake, I'm leaving. But just know this shit isn't over. Business is business and when you fuck me over, you're fucking with all of us. Your ass is grass." I spat before slamming the door shut and walking away. My blood boiled as I hopped in my blue Mercedes and dialed my accomplice on speed dial.

"Yeah?" They answered. "I'm comin' over there. That bitch fucked up. Not only is his ass is on the line, but so is that bitch Simone too." I explained angrily. "Good. The plan is in session. Come on over and let's talk." My accomplice reminded me. "Yes, the plan is in session." I said with a smile. I quickly hung up the phone and headed off to my destination. It was now time for things to come into full effect.

Sweetz

Sunday morning, the day to give God some time and to spend time with your family. That use to be my routine when I was younger, but after I turned fourteen and moved to Detroit, things changed. I mean I always had a relationship with my Lord and Savior, but things have just been shaky these past six years...Until now. Today, I decided to go out to church and brunch with the infamous Jayden this morning. The whole experience today was life changing. My whole perspective has changed. I want the best life for my baby and I, and I want to be the woman living on the right path.

Over these few weeks, Jayden and I have become closer than I imagined. Even though Simone moved out into her new house, I'm not alone like I thought I would be. Jayden spends every night and morning with me. He's been there for me in my time of need, and he treats me so good. I never knew there could be a man so dedicated to me, and can make me feel so happy and so alive.

On a daily basis, Jayden comes over to cook me dinner, watch movies with me, and lay in the bed and cuddle up with me at night. The topic of sex has never been brought up and he has never made one move. Maybe it's his age and maturity, or maybe it's because I'm so use to the sexual relationship I always had with Smooth, anything else is rare. Whatever it may be, I came to realize that Jayden is really a good man.

After taking a nice warm shower, I slipped into my red and white floral print maxi dress, pulled my hair into a bun, and slid my feet into my red satin slippers. During this whole pregnancy, all I wear is maxi dresses since it's feminine and perfect for my baby bump. I always dreamed of sharing this pregnancy with Smooth, but that is only a dream. Life has a funny way of slapping your ass out of a dream world into a harsh reality.

I quickly was reminded that things are finally getting better for me when walked into my living room, only to see Jayden sitting on my couch, looking as innocent as a child. Jayden's caramel skin illuminated under the dim light, while he was dressed down in his black muscle shirt and his black sweat pants. I could see his chiseled muscles a mile away, and the tattoos on his arms were just so appeasing.

"You're not bad for a thirty-five year old." I joked, while heading over to him. "Not too bad huh?" He laughed. "Baby I'm amazing for a thirty-five year old." He continued, before holding me in his arms and planting a soft kiss on my lips. "Mmm...Oh really. You're amazing huh? Why don't you give me another amazing kiss." I smiled flirtatiously. "That's not a problem." He said in his deep and sexy voice.

Gently grabbing the back of my neck, Jayden pulled me in closer, laid his soft pink lips onto mine, and began exchanging his tongue with mine in our deep kiss.

I closed my eyes and enjoyed the pleasure this man was giving me off just one kiss, but was quickly interrupted by my cell phone ringing. Jayden quickly pulled away. "I guess you need to go answer that baby." "Ugh...I guess so." I hopped off the couch, mad at the world and grabbed my cell phone off the kitchen counter. I looked at the screen only to see a 313 area code. Something I haven't seen in a long time. Who is this?

"Hello." I answered anxiously. "Well hello stranger...You just poof and disappeared with my niece or nephew like it was nothing huh?" The voice of Liyah trailed through my phone. I quickly let out a sigh of relief. "Oh Liyah, you had me going for a minute. I didn't know who was calling me." I replied. "Mmmhmm...So how you been missy? You and Krazy just dipped out on all of us like it was nothing." She continued, causing me to laugh in response.

"I've been great, leaving Michigan was the best thing for both me and Simone." I said exuberantly. "Hmm...I guess. I don't think Smooth would've like the fact that you just packed ya' shit up and left while carrying his baby. You made a move that is just so disrespectful to a hot boy. Smooth at that! "She jabbed, causing me to instantly get infuriated.

"I don't give a damn what Smooth thinks! As far as I'm concerned when he poof and disappeared for two to three months, he lost all rights of having the title as the father of my child. I 'am the mother and the father of my baby and I will be damned to have you call me and try to question my judgments and decisions. With all due respect, I don't think you have the right to call and chastise me, acting like you are his damn spokesperson. If this is what you are trying to do every time you call me, then don't bother calling me at all Liyah. Just like how I removed Smooth out of my life, I can remove your ass too." I snapped.

"You might want to watch who you are talking to." She started. "No child, you might want to watch who you are talking to and you need to re-evaluate yourself before ever calling me again." I cut her off. "Matter of fact, don't you ever call me again Liyah. Goodbye." I hung up, angry to the point of tears.

How dare she try to call and undermine me like that! Smooth has no say in my world anymore, and his spokesperson sure as hell won't either. So many emotions hit me all at once. I was beyond infuriated and hurt at the fact that I'm trying to move on with my life, yet the past always try to haunt me with Smooth. Why?

"Baby...Are you ok?" Jayden asked while heading towards me. I could feel my insides turning from this anger and pain. I couldn't even open my mouth to answer him. All I could do was drop down to my knees and cry. It was one of those painful cries where I open my mouth and nothing comes out, instead I just cry harder and harder. Dropping down to his knees, Jayden pulled me into his arms and held me tightly in his arms to help console me.

"I-I-I...I'm just so tired of Smooth and his shit popping back up. I worked so hard to change and get a new life. He was the one who left me...He left me...He left me and our child. And I'm the one in the wrong! Am I wrong for wanting to do something for myself? Ever since I was fuckin' fourteen it has been all about Smooth. What Smooth wants, and what Smooth needs. Do this for Smooth, take care of Smooth. But damnit what about me? What about La'nay? Not Sweetz, the girl who is dating Smooth. What about La'nay? Nobody gave a damn about me when Smooth just poof and disappeared on me. No one said shit to me. No sympathy, no nothing. But when I leave and try to go get my shit together, try to start a new life, they want to come and throw shit up in my face. Fuck that! I'm not having it...I'm-" I cried.

"Shhh..." Jayden cut me off by placing his finger to my lips. "You are not wrong. It is all about you and your baby. Don't let anyone change that. Smooth was the asshole that walked away from a beautiful woman and the responsibility of being a father." He started.

"Your past is your past and is not an indicator of your present and future. You always remember that La'nay. You are not alone. I'm here for you and the baby because I care deeply. Smooth couldn't step up and be a man, so now it's time for a real man to step up and be there for you." Jayden explained, wiping my tears from my eyes. The last words he said lingered in my head, I do want a real man in my life... A real man for not only me, but for my baby. I looked up into his eyes, and at that moment I realized that it was now time for me to make that move.

"Jayden..." I muttered. "I want you to be the main man in my life. Can you be that real man for me?" I asked softly, as another tear strolled down my face. Taking my hand and placing it up to his heart, Jayden's hazel eyes penetrated my soul.

"Baby, you don't even have to ask. You said that you wanted me to be the main man in your life. That is all you had to say, whatever you want and need, I will always be willing to give to you baby. As it is said, as it is so baby. I'm all yours." He explained, saying the words that touched my soul. Tears cascaded down my cheek as I leaned in, and kissed the new main man in my life.

<u>Simone</u>

Four months has passed, it's now December and things have changed drastically. Sweetz and I are finally twenty, and things are changing for the better. I now live in my house, moved up in the workplace as Torrian's personal assistant, making tons of money, and to top it off I'm dating Jake! Yes, that sexy chocolate man is all mines when I come home, and he takes care of me every night!

Sweetz is now the ultimate church going, happy, loving, and supportive woman basically playing housewife for Jayden. Every time I see them, I start to tear up. They really portray black love to the fullest. I never could understand why people said that black love was beautiful, because my love with Kris was nothing close to beautiful. Yet after witnessing how that man treats her like a real queen, and how she gives her all for her king, I can truly say black love is beautiful when done right.

Trina's "Look Back at Me" blasted in my red and black Mercedes SUV as I was driving to my job. The Versace sunglasses protected my eyes from the bright sun beaming on this December day. After living in Detroit for almost all my life, it is hard to cope with a winter season with no snow. Yet I'm definitely not complaining.

I wouldn't go back to Detroit and live in the Hot Boy scene if you paid me! This is my new life and I love it. I feel invincible, like I'm the rarest and baddest bitch in the game. I go for mine, and I do what I have to do to get it. I fear no one but God, and

144

I'm the real and original Hot Girl.

No one can walk a mile in my shoes, not even for five minutes. Can you say I'm feeling myself? Oh yes, because I do it the best! For the first time in my life I feel empowered, and I love it. A huge smile protruded on my face as I pulled into the parking lot. Life was so good and I know that it is only going to get better, I can feel it.

"Well hello Simone." The voice of Stacey reached me as soon as I stepped into the Lattermoore & Lattermoore office. "Hello, hello, hello there!" I laughed, as I walked towards her office. Over this course of time, Stacey and I have become real close acquaintances. Friends are no such thing in my world, but she was damn near close to it at work.

Both of us were similar in the work world. We would lie, scheme, sleep, and scandal our way to the top. Is it wrong? Yes! But as the saying always goes, it is a dog eat dog world. Eat or get ate! So in this world, Stacey and I were doing some good ass eating, while these dumb broads were losing in this game of making it to the top.

"So how are things coming along?" She asked, while I closed the door to her office, and slipped into the seat in front of her desk. "It's coming...Just trying to work my way to the top. Doing what I can each day at a time." I replied. "I definitely understand. Mr. Lattermoore is working me hard...Literally. In the bedroom and in the work place." She laughed deviously. "Oh really now." I egged her on. "Yes...He is into that weird dominatrix stuff. I feel so horrible when it's done. But hey, if he likes it then I love it! You should see the bonus checks I get after I shove a little strap-on in his ass." Stacey explained, causing us to laugh in unison.

"Wow. He really makes you do that?" I asked appalled. "Yes, sick huh? I tell you those rich business men are really into the weirdest and nastiest things. You would be surprised at what these white-collared millionaires love behind closed doors." She continued, causing me to frown up in disgust.

"That is just by far the most disgusting thing I ever heard, but then again I can believe it." I said still in shock. "Oh yes girly! So how is Torrian treating ya'?" She asked curiously. "Well not like how Mr. Lattermoore is treating your ass." I laughed. "He's not into the crazy side of life. But he just will not leave me alone. He is so damn clingy and wants me to do every damn thing for him. I know I'm his personal assistant but damn...I need a break. I do have a life outside of work you know?" I finished.

"Hmm...I never heard of Torrian being clingy with his personal assistants. But it seems like with you, it's different... He really likes you so much, that it is kind of scary. He talks about you all the time to everyone, and it's just something about the way he looks at you. Like he is...Nevermind." Stacey stopped abruptly.

"Like he is what? Tell me." I said, pushing her to let it out. "It's like he is obsessed with you. It's just scary you know? It's similar to one of those fatal attractions. But Torrian isn't that bad, so I doubt it would get that far." She said, shrugging off her fear. "Yeah, I don't think so." I replied while still in deep thought.

146

Torrian is not that damn crazy? He may seem a little off at times, and claims that he is in love with me, but he is not crazy. The sound of my blackberry going off knocked me out of my deep thought. According to the text message, Torrian needed me to come to his office urgently.

"Speaking of the man himself, here he is." I laughed while jumping out my seat, and heading out of Stacey's office. "I will see you later chica." I finalized, before walking towards Torrian's office down the hall.

"I came as fast as I could Torrian." I said urgently, as I stepped into Torrian's spacious and extravagant office. "Good." He said in a serious tone. "Close the door and close the blinds." He commanded. Without another word said, I followed his commands, and returned back to my stance in front of his desk. "Now take everything off except your heels, and come sit on my desk." He said while observing my body in pure lust. Wow! Did he really just urgently call me in just to have sex? What is wrong with this man? I'm here to work, not to get worked! Yet, as I slipped off my clothes, all I could think about was the bonus check that I was going to receive next week.

"Mmm." He commented, while tracing my curves with his eyes. I slowly walked around the other side of his desk, switching my hips the sexiest way I knew how. After he pushed all the belongings off his desk, I positioned myself on top of his desk, formed the spread eagle, and allowed him to eat an early lunch.

After getting worked, I was now back in my office getting ready to do some real work. I knew that I officially moved up in the marketplace when I got the keys to my new office, right across the hall from Stacey, and down the hall from Torrian. I moved up from the cubicle to the office, and next thing will be from the office, to owning my own damn headquarters!   Stacey and I talked about how we should partner up and start our own business. In this country anything is possible. I don't have to obtain a college degree to own a business. You either sink or swim when it comes to success! When you got the skill and knowledge to run a business, then you got it!

I don't need a professor to tell me something I already know. That would be a waste of my time, and as the Hot Boyz always says, "Time is money and money is time, and I don't have time or money to waste.

"The abrupt knocks on my door interrupted my thought process. "Come in." I shouted from my desk. As soon as the door opened, I automatically locked eyes with the one and only Jake.

Underneath his sexy leather jacket, Jake was dressed in his black Gucci button up, crisp Gucci blue jeans, and some black loafers to pull off his casual attire. Just the sight of my chocolate love, standing in my doorway holding a bouquet of red roses, caused my heart to jump. Jake is truly the man of my dreams.

"Hey love." Jake greeted as he walked up to me, and planted a sweet peck on my lips. "Hey baby. What are you doing here?" I smiled contagiously. "I decided to stop by and treat us to a nice lunch today." He answered, while taking a seat in front of my desk. "I would love that, let me check with Torrian and see if that's ok. I'm pretty sure it wouldn't be a problem though." I said, while grabbing my phone and dialing Torrian's extension.

"Hello." His voiced traveled over the phone. "Hello Mr. Lyles, I'm calling to let you know that I'm going out for lunch. Before I go, is there anything you would like me to do sir?" I asked in my professional manner. "Uhh...You already took care of that. And did a damn good job at it too." Torrian chuckled, causing me to get disgusted at the thought. "Well...I guess not, where are you going to eat at? I should come and join you!" He intruded. "I'm sorry, but Jake is taking me out to eat." I said, breaking him down gently.

"Jake? Your boyfriend Jake is here?" He asked in shock. "Yes, he is." I concurred. "Ugh! I don't think that's a good idea Simone." Torrian flipped, in pure disgust. "What!" I started to get loud, but realized Jake was sitting there with all eyes on me. "What do you mean?" I finished in a calmer tone. "You have a lot of work to do, I need you. So you can't go." He replied triumphantly.

"I can't go? You are really telling me 'No' to going out to eat?" I said puzzled at this decision. "Yes. As a bosses order, I'm telling you that you can't go out to eat. I guess you better order in!" He commanded, and hung up in my face before I could even mutter out a word.

I couldn't believe he would flip out on me like that. This was the first time Torrian would pull a stunt like this, yet I had a feeling that it wouldn't be the last. "What did he say?" Jake asked, with a raised eyebrow. "He said no. I have a lot of work to do so I have no time to go out and eat. But we can eat in baby." I said, placing a smile on my face to cover up my anger.

"What the hell! I'm not liking your boss Simone. He works you like a Hebrew slave, and makes you answer to his every beg and call." Jake began, ranting in irritation. "You are too young, and too beautiful. I understand you want to make this money, but baby...There are other ways. I can help you out if you needed money that bad. My woman should never want for nothing. I know we are just dating, but when that day comes..." I quickly placed a halt to his lecture.

"That day? Jake baby, you need to pump your breaks. It's one thing to express how you feel, but it's another to be lecturing me. You are my man, not my Father. Get that straight. You know me, but clearly not well enough. I'm not depending on no man! I did that once and I promised myself that I never will do that again. You are out doing your thing, making money, so let me do mine." I explained. "Okay Simone. I'm not going to argue with you today. I'm not." Jake surrendered, looking out the window. I could tell by how his jaw was locking, that he was nowhere near amused. Yet, I'm not the one to back down.

"It's nothing to argue about Jake. It is what it is. This is my job, this is what I do. If you don't like it, then you know what you're going have to do." I spewed. "Oh really Simone! And what is that?" Jake asked, raising his voice. "Get the stepping! That is what you will have to do." I said harshly, causing Jake to abruptly jump out of his chair, and stand in front of my desk. "I have to get the stepping Simone?" He yelled, knocking the vase of roses off my desk.

I never seen him so angry, yet it was something so sexy about him getting so shook at the thought of losing me. Kris was never like that, it was always me being the one scared to lose him. Now I finally have it the other way around.

"Foreal Simone? You are really going to make me get the stepping huh? No, that's not happening. I'm not losing you over some shitty ass job that you spend more time working at. Practically babysitting some little ass boy who can't be a man and do his own shit." Jake yelled louder.

"Jake calm down. We are in my workplace, there is no need to argue here. How about we talk about this later." I said calmly. "No fuck that!" He spat, in pure anger.

"Fuck this place, Fuck talking later. I'm not going to let this ruin us. What the hell is the point in standing here, and arguing about some bitch ass job? You want me to get the stepping when it comes to your job? Fine, I will do that. Enough fucking said!" He continued, before grabbing his leather jacket, and storming out my office.

I sat in my office, in pure shock. How the hell did I just let Torrian come in-between Jake and I? I had to make things right. I had to do something. Jake is my heart, I knew from day one that this man was the man for me. Why would I let anything come in-between that? Not this job, not this money, not even this chase to the top could ruin what I have with Jake. With a quickness, I ran out my office and followed him into the parking lot.

"Jake. Don't leave baby. I don't want this to ruin us." I

explained, out of breath from trying to run in these damn pumps. "Oh really?" He fumed. "Yes really." I said, as I placed my hands gently behind his neck. "I don't want to lose you Jake. You mean so much to me baby. I'm so happy to be yours. I wanted you from day one, and now I finally got you baby...So why would I lose you over nothing?" I explained.

"Baby, I..." I paused, and stared into his deep black eyes. "You what baby ? " He asked, finally showing me some compassion. "I love you." I confessed. "I love you too Simone." He replied. Grabbing me by my waist, Jake pulled me into a warm and inviting kiss and at that moment, I felt myself get weak in the knees. Damn, I guess I'm really in love.

<u>Kris</u>

"But I love you baby." The voice of Samya trailed behind me, while I sat on the edge of my bed placing my black timbs on my feet. It was four in the morning and it was time to rise and grind. I laughed at the thought of love. Love ain't shit but a whole bunch of random and fictitious emotions. I love no one but my damn self! So all that stuff she is talking can kick rocks.

"Do you have to leave me baby? " She whined. "Don't act stupid, you know I have to go out and grind." I said, turning around and looking her directly in the eyes. "But baby..." She cried, throwing herself onto me. "Get off me girl...You know I have to go. Stop acting so damn clingy." I said in disgust, while pushing her off of me. I hated clingy females more than anything in this world.

Although I have a desire for power and control, this clingy-shit is not flattering. For a female to be my main chick, you have to be a strong and bad ass woman. To hold the title, you have to be a woman who can hold it down in the streets, and still be my heart at the same time. You have to be a real woman...A woman like Krazy.

The thoughts of my growing pains began to haunt me as I hopped off the bed, and threw on my hoodie. I grabbed my keys, hopped into my black escalade, and drove off to my destination.

As I puffed on my blunt full of the best South African Kush, the sound of Yung L.A's "Ain't I" remix, blasted heavily in my car. At the stoplight, I took a real good look at myself in the mirror. My gray eyes were low and emotionless, I'm over here with a beard like Rick Ross, and my braids that use to be shoulder length, are now down to my lower back. I could barely recognize my own damn self. I turned into someone I never wanted to become. I became a disloyal, conniving, backstabbing, and lying *Deceiver*. I 'am the grimiest of the grimiest, and the lowest of the low. I 'am everything a Hot Boy should not be. Yet then again, I'm not a Hot Boy, and a Hot Boy is not me.

I lost everything and everyone close to me. I lost Krazy, the woman who was my heart, my love, and my family. She was the only person in the world who knew me better than anyone else.

She was my family and I was family to her. I loved her with all my heart, yet when the streets were calling, I had to let her go.

I lost Mike, the "little brother" in the Hot Boy clique, killed by the same niggas that I'm affiliated with. I know he is turning over in his grave right now, and was now kissing the ass of the same guys who killed him.

Then I lost Smooth, my best friend, my right hand man...Gone. No one knows where he is or if he is even alive. Smooth just poof and disappeared leaving me with so many questions left unanswered. Shit, I guess that's all a part of my journey to the top.

When Killa' Mike died, the Hot Boyz died. Nothing will ever be the same again, no matter what happens or who comes back. I'm now the leader of the H-Block gang, Detroit chapter. J-ro took over Chicago sector, leaving me to run the streets of Detroit. My mission is finally accomplished. Yet why do I feel so lonely?

Jake

After a nice long session of lovemaking, I began to drift off to sleep with Simone's warm body wrapped under my arms. The tranquil silence and the cool breeze coming from my open window relaxed my mind and body, which was truly needed after a rough day of work. Yet my peaceful and serene sleep came into a world crashing end, as soon as Simone's blackberry went off loudly throughout the room.

Jumping out of my arms, Simone quickly grabbed her phone. "Hello...Yes sir! I will come in right away." She said urgently into the phone. Come in right away? I rolled over only to be greeted with "5:00 A.M" on my digital clock. What the hell?

"Simone...Why are you going in to work, at five in the morning?" I asked half sleep. "It is an important meeting coming up this week that Torrian needs help with. He wants me to come in as soon as possible today. He really needs my help baby." She explained, as she slipped into her sweater dress. "Yeah. He needs you alright." I mumbled.

I knew how she felt about me lecturing about her job, so I decided to back off. "I will be back baby." She smiled, before pecking me on the lips and walking out. It was something about that little punk Torrian that made me sick to my stomach. I knew something wasn't right, so me being an inquisitive person, I'm going to find out. As soon as I heard Simone pull off, I grabbed my cell phone and called up one of my connects.

"Hello. Who is this?" The deep voice answered. "It's me,

Black." I replied. "Oh, hello boss." He greeted with the upmost respect. "What's going on?" He asked. "I need you to do a job for me. Do you know Torrian Lyles?" I interrogated. "The Lattermoore's spoiled ass nephew?" He embarked. "Yes, that little weak ass lame. He is fucking with my girl at the job, and I'm not liking that. I need you to...You know keep a close eye on him, do some research, and bring back the info for me. You got that?" I commanded.

"Yes boss." He replied. "Good. All I ask of you is to do your job and do it well. If you fuck up, your life will be fucked up. And no one will see your ass ever again. You understand me?" I threatened. "Yes sir. I will get on it right now boss." He said urgently before hanging up and getting to business.

If this little, spoiled ass wimp think he can fuck around and take advantage of my girl, he has another thing coming. I'm not one to be fucked with. If you are fucking with me and mine, you will fuck around and lose your life! I don't talk, I don't fight, and I for damn sure ain't wasting time to argue. If you fuck up, I will merk you. Point. Blank. Period.

<u>Simone</u>

Another session, and another day of doing all I can to make it to the top. Two weeks has passed and here I 'am giving my all for a little piece of money and independence. Yet am I really gaining independence, when I'm depending on an estranged man to give me a raise? So many thoughts clouded my head as I laid in the backseat of Torrian's car, watching him heave over me.

Sweat was dripping all over him like he was really doing something. Psssh, the nerve of this man to even think he can put it down when it comes to sex! "Uggggggghhhh! Yes...You like this baby?" He growled. "Ooo...Mmmhmm daddy...I love it daddy!" I said faking a moan. "Damn. I love you girlllllll" He screeched, as he finally reached his peak. Finally he was done, because shit, a girl was getting tired of lying here.

"Woo girl. You know you are the best." He said, while trying to catch his breath. I smiled in return while I slipped into my dress, leaving my panties for him to smell, just as he requested. Weird? Yes, but hey if that's what he wants, then that's what he gets.

As we stepped out the car into the parking lot, I couldn't help but notice this black Cadillac that I've been seeing for the past two weeks, parked not too far from us. With the windows being a presidential black tint, it was hard to see who was sitting in there, but I had a feeling it was someone following us. But then again, maybe I'm just overreacting.

"So, same time tomorrow?" Torrian asked, interrupting my thoughts. "Yes of course." I replied. "Good." He ended, before pecking me on the lips. "See you later Simone." He smiled. "Ok Torrian." I smiled back, before heading to my car. I had officially one hour to shower, and get ready to see my baby Jake tonight. I can't wait!

Jake

"And she did what?" I yelled angrily through the phone. I could not believe the shit I was hearing. My baby is fuckin' that lame ass for extra money! This whack ass excuse of a man was dicking my girl down whenever he wanted huh? He must think he can get away with this shit...but that's not happening. I was infuriated at the thought of someone else having sex with my girlfriend. Yet I knew all about Simone, more than she assumed. I can't be fooled. I'm too smart for that.

"Wait, there is more boss." My worker chipped in, adding more fuel to the fire. "What more could there be?" I asked coldly. "You have to see for yourself. This nigga is sick and twisted as hell. We have a video to show you." He explained. I could feel my blood beginning to boil from the anger that was spreading throughout my body. "A video? Bring that shit over here right now. No questions asked. Bring your ass!" I commanded before hanging up.

Within ten minutes, my worker K-row, walked in with a video tape in his hand, as well as a folder of what appeared to be pictures. "Boss, you are not going to believe this shit if I told you. You have to see this for yourself!" He exclaimed, while setting up the TV and the VCR player. I had a feeling that this was going to be something I couldn't even imagine, so I sparked my Cuban Cigar to help be some assistance in calming me down.

"You were recording them?" I asked. "Nope. This is the video we found in his house." He replied, placing me into shock. "In his house?" "Yes boss...You have to see for yourself before I can explain further. Just watch for yourself." He reassured me. "Well let me see this shit then." I demanded impatiently. "Ok boss." He agreed, and began to play the tape.

The first scene was of Simone, but the setting was in her personal bedroom of her home. Due to the quality of this video, I could tell that this was a hidden camera, which this nigga placed in her house. But how? I continued to watch various scenes of Simone following her daily routine such as changing clothes, taking a shower, and finally, of her and I having sex! After viewing this, I instantly became full of rage, and everything in sight became a shade of red.

"This nigga had hidden cameras in her house?" I yelled. "Yes boss. It gets crazier. We found out that he lives across the street from her. But she doesn't know that. He was very discreet on coming and leaving his home. As you can see in the pictures, he has been watching and stalking her, just as much as we were stalking him." K-row began.

"My team and I finally got the chance to get into his house while he was gone, and man, the things we seen! He has a wall of photos of her, collections of her panties, and videos of her. He is beyond obsessed. It's sickening." He ended in disgust. I couldn't even respond to none of this shit. I was beyond infuriated. "What are you going to do boss?" He asked sincerely.

"You know what has to be done K-row. But I just have to think of how. This nigga has gone far beyond disrespecting not only Simone, but me. No one disrespects me. No one! So I will call you, when I'm ready. Until then, your work is done. You may leave." I said, dismissing him. "Yes boss." K-row said, before obeying my wishes. As I sat alone in my office, puffing on my Cuban cigar, I began thinking of a master plan.

Sweetz

"Can you believe it? We made it a whole year, through all this, and look how drastically we changed." I said, as we sat at my kitchen counter over a glass of sparkling grape juice. It was New Year's Eve, and all the magic would be hosted at my condo. Jayden and Jake were out running errands, while we waited for the guest to arrive. "I know right? Things are so different now, but then again, it's for the best." Simone smiled. "Cheers to that!" I joked, causing us to laugh in unison.

"And it's only going to get better." She continued on. "As long as we have each other, there is nothing else to worry about. You are family Sweetz. You are all I have. No matter what goes on with our life, with men, with our careers, and our paths of life. We are all we got." "Aww..." was all I could say as I hugged her. She was right, we were truly all we had. No matter what went on, Simone was not only my best friend, she my ride or die.

The hard knocks on the door were the only thing interrupting our "sister to sister" moment. I quickly broke the hug, and greeted my guest at the door. Most of which, were Jayden and Jake's family members and close friends. Although they were not present, the show must go on.

<u>Simone</u>

Hours passed and Jayden and Jake were nowhere to be found. I scanned around the room, trying to find Sweetz. If someone knew where they would be, I knew she would be the best person to ask; since she always kept tabs on her man. It didn't take me long to locate her, since her pregnant ass was in the kitchen, tearing up some gourmet chicken.

"Where the hell is Jake and Jayden?" I asked Sweetz. "I don't even know. This is their family members here at this party, and they are nowhere to be found." She replied, as we watched everyone counting down. "10...9...8...7..." The crowd began to shout gleefully, as I began to get worried. "6...5...4...3..." Where the hell is he? "2..." What the hell...

"1." The voice of Jake traveled in my ear. I immediately turned around to see him standing there. "Baby! I missed you." I said, as I hugged him tightly. "I missed you too baby." He replied, before placing a sweet kiss on my lips. "Mmm...I missed those kisses too baby." I naughtily remarked, not paying attention to the crowd going crazy off the New Year. "Close your eyes." He commanded. "Why?" I asked, scrunching my face up. "Just do it girl." He laughed. "Ok fine." I hesitantly agreed and closed my eyes.

I could feel him holding my left hand, and next thing I knew, I felt him put a ring on my finger. Is he really doing this?

"Open your eyes baby." He said calmly. I quickly opened my eyes, and was greeted to huge rock on my finger. "Baby!" I screamed, as I jumped on him and kissed that man, giving him my all. "So I take that as a yes huh?" He chuckled. "Yes! Oh hell yes!" I exclaimed, while still in his arms and my legs wrapped around his torso. Everyone clapped and awed at our engagement. "I'm so happy for you girl." Sweetz yelled out from the crowd. "Shit, I'm happy for my damn self." I gleamed with joy. "You ready to go baby?" Jake laughed. "Hell yes...We have some celebrating to do." I answered, while jumping off him.

This was one of the happiest days of my life. I was now about to be Mrs. Simone Shamir, the wife of the sexy Jake Shamir. Damn, life can't get any better than this! After drinking in celebration to my engagement, Jake and I headed to his house, and began to get it in.

With my legs wrapped around his shoulders, his right hand gently choking my neck, and the left hand caressing one of my thighs, Jake continued to pound my pussy like no tomorrow. "This pussy is mine! Tell me it's mine." He said in the sexiest voice. "Mmm...It's yours daddy." I moaned full of pure pleasure. "Mmm...Tell me it's mine baby, and not that nigga Torrian's." He said, shocking the hell out of me. "Huh?" was all I could say as he began to choke and pound me harder. "Mmmhmm...You think I didn't know about that baby." He began talking, while pounding my pussy harder and harder with each stroke.

"It's ok baby. Cause you are all mine. This pussy is all mine, and he will never get another taste of this pussy ever again. That nigga can't do it like me. I know he can't. Does he do you like this?" He asked, as he pulled out, flipped me over, and shoved his thick dick inside my little pussy. I screamed in pure pleasure, as he grabbed my hair, and fucked me like no other.

"Hmm...Does he do it like this baby?" He said coldly, as he thrusted harder inside me and smacked my ass violently. "Noooooooooooooooooooooo." I cried. "I knew it...That nigga will never be me, and he will never have this pussy again." He said as he leaned in closer to me. "Mark my words baby." He whispered in my ears, as he began to pump me into a mind blowing orgasm. Yet that didn't stop him. Jake continued to control and man handle this pussy until my ass passed out.

He put it on me so good, that I couldn't even move out the bed the next day. Being the gentleman he was, Jake carried me to my awaiting bubble bath that he ran for me, and pampered me the whole day. Damn, no one could tell me that this wasn't love. If they did I would smack them dead, because this was truly the man for me. Despite me cheating on him for my career, he still forgave me, and treated me like a queen. Now what man does that?

As I headed to work the next morning, I couldn't help but smile at the thought of becoming a married woman. There had to be changes that needed to be made. All I've been doing here in California was committing deceiving acts; sleeping with my boss to receive a bigger salary, constantly lying to the man I love, and scamming my way to the top. Today I was going to finally get rid of it all. I'm going to walk into this office, and let Torrian know that I'm done. I'm tired of his shit, tired of being his sex toy, and tired of working here. I was officially done with this lifestyle. It's time to become that woman Jake needs as a wife.

With my mind made up, and determination flowing through my blood, I walked into the office ready to crush Torrian's little heart. Yet, I was greeted by a storm of detectives and police officers. As soon as I stepped in, all eyes were on me. The conversation between Stacey and one of the detectives was placed to a sudden halt when I walked in. The look of shock on her face led me to believe that whatever is going on here, must be directed towards me... But what the hell is going on here?

"Are you Simone Simmons?" A tall brown skin detective asked with urgency. "Yes." I answered hesitantly. "We need to take you down to the office to ask you a couple of questions." The detective began. "Questions? Questions about what?" I cut him off, in confusion. "Questions regarding the death of Torrian Lyles." He answered, leaving me in pure shock.

My heart sunk, as I dropped down in the closest seat next to me. I couldn't believe that Torrian was dead. "It was a brutal homicide and we need you to help us solve this case." The detective continued. "You need me to help solve this case?" I asked puzzled. How the hell can I help solve a case, if I didn't even know that there was a murder in the first place?

"Yes, maybe there is something you could tell us which could be very helpful for the case." He explained further. "I guess." I agreed, tired of going back and forward with him. Out of all the murders I committed with Kris, never have I been so worried to become a prime suspect like I' am now.

As I sat in the backseat of the police car, my mind wandered, trailing over the memories of my days as a being the girlfriend of a Hot Boy. There were so many men that I killed in cold blood, never have I thought twice about getting caught. Yet here I' am getting treated like a suspect for the murder of a man, who I actually had some type of relationship with. So many thoughts filled my head as I sat in the investigation room, getting prepared to get questioned by the detectives.

"I'm sure you don't understand why you are here Ms. Simmons. But I'm here to ensure that you will have some understanding by the end of this process. My name is Detective Gutierrez." A tall, creamy tanned man, with deep chocolate brown eyes, explained calmly. "This is my partner, who you've already met at the office, Detective Brown." He finished. "Ok, so why am I here?" I asked staring directly in Detective Gutierrez's eyes.

Silence swept over the room immediately after I asked a simple question. The two detectives looked at each other, as if something was too disturbing to even state. "What the hell is goin' on? Can you answer my damn question? Why am I here? How can I help solve a murder case if I didn't even know there was a murder present?" I began to spew out of irritation.

"What type of relationship did you and Mr. Lyles have outside of work?" Detective Brown asked as he leaned against the wall observing me. "What the...What does that have to do with anything?" I said, in pure confusion. "Just answer the question Ms. Simmons." Detective Gutierrez firmly commanded.

"How about you tell me what does this have to do with anything?" I remarked, with a full blown attitude.

"How about we try this again, did you and Mr. Lyles have some type or relationship outside of work?" Detective Brown rephrased. "Yes, we did." I answered nonchalantly. "Was it Sexual?" Detective Gutierrez threw in. "And if it was, why does it matter?" I scoffed. "Why does it matter?" Detective Gutierrez laughed, as he stood up with a thick manila folder in his hand. "It matters a whole lot when you see this shit." He snapped, as he violently threw the folder onto the table.

I quickly opened up the folder, only to see the first photograph displaying some type of collage. A collage of over thousands of pictures of me on the wall! "What the hell is this?" I asked, as I stared at this photo in shock. "This is what we found in his house." Detective Brown answered. "In his house..." I said as I trailed off in deep thought, trying to understand this mess.

The voices of the Detectives began to fade in and out, as I flipped through the photos. The photos revealed that Torrian was not only stalking me, but he was obsessed with me! He had a collection of my panties next to his bed, tons of candid snapshots of me doing daily activities, and a pair of binoculars facing my bedroom from across the street. Yet my stomach churned at the sight of the picture revealing the homicide.

Torrian sat duct taped to his loveseat, facing what appears to be the TV playing a video of me in the bedroom! His mouth was taped shut, yet his eyeballs were plucked out his eye sockets. The sight was so gruesome; I couldn't stand to look at the picture anymore.

How the hell could someone do that to him? Yet, why the hell was he so obsessed with me? I didn't know what to think, what to feel, or how to react. A part of me wanted to cry, yet a part of me wanted to just say "That's what he fuckin' gets"...But it's still not right for him to die like that. "We don't think you are a suspect Ms. Simmons. From your reaction, you were clearly unaware that all of this was going on." Detective Gutierrez said compassionately. "Do you think there is anyone that you may know who would do this, in order to protect you?" Detective Brown asked.

At that moment, the only person who came to mind was Jake. "*I knew it...That nigga will ever be me, and he will never have this pussy again*"... "*Mark my words baby.*" I immediately replayed the words that Jake whispered in my ears, two nights ago in my head. Yet, Jake is a good, wholehearted Realtor, not a cold blooded killer.

The homicide of Torrian was nice and clean, not messy and full of passion. It was clearly a job of a professional, or a serious notorious gang member who has done this for a while. It couldn't be Jake, and shit Kris was out of sight, and out of mind. I quickly looked up at the detectives hovering over me, allowed my tears to continue to flow, to help gain some sympathy, and answered "No."

After hours of being in the Police Station, I was finally out and done with this Torrian madness. The detectives believed me when I said that I had no one connected to this murder, and was now led to believe that his ex-girlfriend was his murderer. Yet from the pit of my stomach, I knew who killed Torrian. I didn't want to believe that I knew, so I decided to come home, and wash away these deceiving acts. It was time to start off fresh, as if none of this ever happened.

CHAPTER 5: WHEN IT ALL FALLS DOWN

Sweetz

"Mommy! Mommy!" The sweet voice of my two-year-old son greeted me to a new morning. I rolled over in the bed and opened my eyes, only to see the beautiful toffee colored face of my baby boy Mi'quel. His nickname was Little Mike, just like his late Uncle.

Looking at him was like looking at Killa' Mike. From his cute little nose, down to his deep dimples, and that cute baby smile, was just like his Uncle Mike. Yet those penetrating honey colored eyes, and his curly black hair reminded me that he was truly Smooth's son.

"Hey baby...You want to get in the bed with Mommy and Daddy?" I said enthused as he tumbled into the bed between Jayden and I. He instantly began tapping Jayden on the shoulder, ready to play a round of play fight. "Hey big boy! You're ready for a game of play-fight huh?" Jayden asked, as he pulled Mi'quel on top of him and began playing. I smiled at the sight of the two loves of my life. This was our morning routine before we ate breakfast each day. These two people were the reason why I craved to wake up each morning. There is no other man that could be a better father figure to Mi'quel, and better husband to me than Jayden. Jayden is the only man that can satisfy my wants, my needs, and my desires.

As the two played their game of "Play Fight", I began to head downstairs and make breakfast. So many things have changed in two years, other than my age and the year being 2011. At 22, Simone and I were both wives and mothers, playing housewife to prominent and successful men in California. Our past of being a Hot Boyz girlfriend was buried six feet beneath us, and each day I'm thankful for making that one drastic move to L.A.

I look back at the days of living under the microscope of Smooth; not being able to trust anyone, living in fear of being in danger, and I realized that a lifestyle like that is no way for anyone to live. Sure the rewards consisting of the money, the cars, the clothes and the material items are enticing, yet at what price?

So much blood was shed, so many loved ones gone, and so many friends turned into foes...No one could be trusted. Yet you live your life like you are under a microscope, knowing that one day you were bound to die fast. Is it really worth it?

Every time I look at Mi'quel, I see the face of Killa' Mike and think how he could have gone another route in life. At seventeen years old, he should have been in school, getting an education. Yet he followed the footsteps of his big brother Smooth, chasing after the thrown of power and fast money, and ended up losing his life. Tears began to flow down my face as I continued to fix breakfast and reflect over my growing pains. Yet the sounds of Mi'quel's pitter patter coming down the hallway caused me to quickly wipe my tears away, and get back to the present day. I'm a mother and a wife now. Life is too good to dwell on my haunting past, as the saying goes "I'm too blessed to be stressed!"

After enjoying my normal family time, it was time to run errands and make moves. With my hair pulled back into a low ponytail under my pink and black L.A fitted, I slipped into my grey sweat pants that hung off my hips, revealing the butterfly tattoo on my right hipbone. I quickly threw on a light pink tee and some Nike sneakers to match my casual attire. Even in my "Momma gear" I was still sexy as hell!

"I have to go run some errands, so make sure Mi'quel takes a nap in another hour." I explained, as I walked back into the living room where Jayden and Mi'quel were watching SpongeBob on the couch. "Mmm, you're leaving me looking sexy like that?" Jayden said, as he licked his luscious lips, eying every curve of my body. I instantly got turned on by the sight of him. Damn, the things I would do to that man....Might mess around and work on baby number two.

"Yes, I'm leaving you, looking sexy like this." I laughed, as I walked over to them. "I'm sorry love, but I have to go! Mi'quel give me mommy a hug and kiss goodbye." I continued. "Ok mommy." Mi'quel said, as he jumped up and ran over to me. I embraced him tightly, taking in the scent of his Johnson and Johnson cocoa butter lotion. "I love you baby...You be a good boy for daddy ok?" I stated softy as I pecked him on the cheek. "I wuv you too mommy!" He replied sweetly and ran back over to Jayden.

My heart was instantly melted and I was overwhelmed with joy. Never have I loved someone as much as I loved my baby Mi'quel. I always thought that nothing could be stronger than the love I had with Smooth, but now I learned what love really was all about. There is truly nothing stronger than the bond between a mother and her son, I can tell you that much.

"So what about me?" Jayden complained, as he sat on the couch, snapping me out of my loving daze. "Can a brotha' at least get a hug, a kiss, or somethin' before his woman leaves to run errands?" He continued, causing me to laugh. "Aww, come here you big baby!" I exclaimed, as I widely opened my arms, inviting him in. "Yes...I'm a big baby so what!" He joked, as he walked over and was embraced by my love. I gave Jayden a kiss good-bye, grabbed my Fendi bag, and hopped into my SUV.

The music of Drake blasted throughout my car as I strolled down the street, dialing Simone's number on my cell phone. "Hello." She answered politely. "Hey missy..." I greeted. "Ugh! You again." She laughed. "Shut up heffa'! Don't act like you don't want to talk to me." I exclaimed. "Yeah, I guess...What do you want trick?" She asked. "I want yo' ass to throw on some clothes, tell Jake to watch little Jake, and escape with me for a moment." I explained. "It's mommy's day out, so bring your ass outside!" I commanded, as I pulled up in front of her house. "Oh so you running things huh?" She said sarcastically. "Hell yeah...Now bring your ass, I'm outside." I replied before hanging up.

Within five minutes, Simone walked outside dressed in her red BEBE sweat pants, a white t-shirt, and some matching Nike running shoes. Even in her "Mommy gear," Simone still looked stunning. Her hair was pulled up in a high bun, revealing the "Krazy" tattoo that was designed in cursive, on the back of her neck. Her chocolate brown skin complexion was purely radiant. Never have I witnessed this woman glowing like I did today.

"Well hello there!" She beamed, showing off her pearly whites. "Hello,hello,hello." I joked, as I greeted her with a hug. "And why are you so happy today?" I asked out of curiosity. "Girl, how can I not be happy?" She replied. "I'm married to the man of my dreams, I have a beautiful son by this man, and we live in a perfect house, in a perfect town. My best friend lives down the street from me, in her perfect house, with her adorable son, and a loving and progressive man of God." Simone explained.

"La'nay, we have come a long way and I love it. Call me crazy, but the best thing we did for us was to run away from our past and never look back. Our lives are perfect and I know for sure it's going to remain that way. Hopefully forever." Simone finished, leaving the last sentence to linger in my head.

"Perfect huh?" I chimed in as I began driving to our destination. So many thoughts quickly flooded through my head as we rode to the R&B music on the radio. My life was never close to perfect, from the very first day I was born into this world.

I lived with a mother who allowed my step father to molest me, I moved to Detroit and encountered the world of violence, and crime, and I lived my life under a man who was the head of a notorious gang, that corrupted many lives. I sacrificed everything that I had and who I was for a man, who in the end left me high and dry. Yet, here I 'am now... Living what is finally what we would call "Perfect".

"They say nothing in life is perfect, yet I don't believe that La'nay." Simone blurted out, interrupting my deep thoughts. I knew she could sense my uneasiness to her previous comment of our life being perfect. She must have sensed my concern by how she just said the words to oppose my thoughts. I felt like she was reading my mind, like she was in my head hearing my private thoughts.

"I don't believe that shit La'nay." She repeated, snapping me back into her conversation. "Who can say what's perfect when they haven't experienced hell and corruption themselves? If they haven't had the ugliest and lowest things in life, how can they say that nothing in life is perfect? What we been through was nowhere near perfect La'nay. It was like a life of hell. Yet here we are in heaven, living life that is perfect and pure. So I don't believe that phrase that nothing in life is perfect. Cause damnit, our life today is perfect." She explained passionately.

As I parked the car in the parking lot of the shopping mall, I let out a heavy sigh and looked Simone in her tear filled eyes. I wanted to really believe and agree with her, but something in the pit of my stomach wouldn't allow me to.

"Simone, I understand what you are saying. I really do..." I stopped myself in mid-sentence. I could see the life in her eyes. This was something she really believed and had so much faith in. I didn't want to ruin her happiness. I couldn't let myself pop her bubble. I knew that all good things must come to an end, but I just didn't know when this good thing would come to an end. Shit, who knows when this will end, or if this will ever end? Why am I so negative, when life is so positive towards me?

"Gurl, let's just go up in this mall and shop til' we drop!" I said with a smile, quickly changing the subject. "Hell yeah! I need to go buy some more shoes and handbags. Oh, and get little Jake some new outfits. He's getting so big!" Simone continued to ramble on and on, but I tuned her out.

As we both stepped out the car and headed into the mall, a huge feeling of relief swept over my body just at the sight of seeing Simone happy. Sometimes it's best to bite your tongue and push certain feelings aside, at the price of the happiness of your loved ones. Yet, am I wrong for ignoring this eerie feeling I have crawling down my spine, just to have a moment of happiness? I guess it's a risk that I will have to take.

<u>Simone</u>

"Baby, I'm hoooooooome!" I exclaimed as I walked into the front door of my home, with my hands filled with shopping bags. "La'nay and I shut that mall down baby...I bought you and Little Jake shitloads of stuff!" I continued talking, as I walked into the living room searching for my family. "Baby, where are you?" I asked as I looked around the empty living room.

Silence remained to float in the air as I slowly began to panic. Usually Jake would always reply to me whenever I announced that I was home. Or at least little Jake would be running to me, asking me to bake him cookies... Yet this evening was a different story.

Fear began to creep over my body, as I traveled all over the lower floor of our home, searching for my husband and my son. What the hell was going on? The sounds of voices finally began to protrude from what appeared to be upstairs. With a quickness, I ran from the kitchen and headed upstairs to the second floor. The voices finally began to get louder and were coming from the direction of Jake's office.

I opened the door to his office urgently, only to witness Jake sitting at his desk, laughing and talking to a mysterious woman. I quickly noticed that this woman was holding my one year old son, who was contently sitting in her lap. The woman's head was turned so I couldn't view her face. All I could see was her smooth cinnamon brown skin, illuminated under her black dressy attire. "What is going on Jake?" I asked abruptly, causing everyone, including my son, to look in my direction.

As soon as the woman looked up at me, I instantly realized who she was. The shopping bags instantly dropped out my hand, as I locked eyes with the woman, who I would never imagine having to cross paths with in my life again. She was Samya, the bitch that I almost killed years ago. The same bitch who I heard was currently dating Kris. So what the hell was she doing in my house?

"What the hell is she doing here?" I asked, as I stared her down. "Baby chill! This is one of my business affiliates Samya Roslyn. She is only here to talk about some new real estate demographics. Samya this is my wife Simone, Simone this is Samya." Jake introduced calmly, yet all I heard was pure bullshit! Business my ass, I knew that bitch wanted to take what was mine. She already took Kris, and now here she is tryin' to get up under my husband and get all goody-goody with my son. I'll be damned!

"Well hello Simone, It is finally nice to meet you. Jake has told me so much about you. You are such a lucky woman, and your son is adorable by the way." Samya said in her sweet yet professional tone. Once again, all I heard was pure bullshit. "Yeah, whateva'. " I spat cruelly. "C'mon Jakey, let's go downstairs and watch bob the builder while mommy makes dinner." I said, as I grabbed my son off of that bitches lap. "Cookies? You make cookies for me mommy?" He suggested sweetly as we began to head towards the door. "Yes baby I will bake cookies." I chuckled, as I left the office and headed downstairs. If it wasn't for my son being there, I would have went the fuck off and showed them a little taste of Krazy. Yet I'm Simone and I'm a mother, so I had to keep my composure and play my role. But it's not over.....Not even by a long shot!

I put little Jake to sleep early and waited until that trifilin' skeezer left, before I walked into Jake's office and started my mess. Knowing me, I'm not the one to let shit go. I might let it slide at that time, but I would definitely come back and finish what was started.

"So you guys were talking about real estate huh Jake?" I said as I leaned against the doorway, staring him down. "Look Simone." Jake sighed. "Samya is my new business affiliate. She will be here a lot more often handling business with me. You already know how I feel about my career. It comes first to me. So whatever little issue you may have with her, you need to suck that shit up and get over it." He continued, placing me in disbelief. Did this Negro just say that I need to suck that shit up and get over it?

"Look, I have some serious contracts that I have to look over right now. I don't have time to go back and forward with you tonight Simone. I really don't! So we can have this little conversation another day. Just let me do my work, and we can talk about this later ok?" Jake explained, while looking down at his papers.

I stood in the doorway in pure shock. Out of the two years that we've been married, Jake has never talked to me like this! As if I was a child. Never have I felt so low and restricted to say anything until now. I stared at him, trying to gather my thoughts. For the first time in my life, I was at a loss for words. This is not who I 'am, I have to say something, I can't back down!

Before I could even open my mouth to say one word, Jake reached over to his work phone and began dialing a number. Yet that wasn't going to stop me, I was determined to get my last word in. "I can't..." I started. "Yeah, Keith...This is Jake calling about the Townsmen residential area." Jake began, shutting down the sentence I was just starting. Anger filled my body as I stormed out his office, and headed to our master bedroom. I couldn't believe he would dismiss me like that!

As I laid in our bed alone, I stared at the white wall to the right of me, and allowed my tears of anger to flow. All that talk of everything in our lives being perfect was now thrown out the window. As of tonight, I would have to eat my words. I knew that this would be the start of something horrible, ruining what I once called "perfect".

<u>Kris</u>

"So what the fuck is this about?" I asked my fellow gang affiliate J-ro as we walked towards the H-block board room. "Why are we having a random ass meeting in the middle of the day?" I continued. "I don't know. It's probably about some serious shit that we need to discuss." J-ro answered nonchalantly.

"Right..." I coined in, as I looked at him dead in the eye. For something so serious, why is this nigga so calm about it? This nigga must think I'm dumb as rocks, but I guess he doesn't know who he is fuckin' with. I'm Kris, the original leader of the Hot Boyz... I'm always ten steps ahead of them. No one can play me for stupid! I had my glock tucked in tightly in my boxers, just in case some shit popped off.

As we walked into the boardroom, my eyes quickly scanned the faces of each member and to my surprise I was greeted by a familiar face. "Well hello Cashmere." I said calmly. "Yo, you know her?" J-ro asked, as he sat down in his seat. "Sure he does. We go way back. Don't' we Kris?" Cashmere beamed. "Yeah, I guess." I replied, as I sat down in my seat. "So what the fuck is goin' on? And why is she here?" I asked, getting right to the point. "Well I guess there is no need for introductions, since you already know this broad." J-ro spoke with a full blown attitude. What the fuck was his problem?

"You have a problem with that nigga?" I blurted out, with my eyes darting at his head. "I'm just saying...But anyway Cash is here because her and her affiliates are goin' to join us as we make this run to L.A." J-ro announced. "Whoa, whoa...What the fuck do you mean Cash and her affiliates? Since when did we let outsiders and their affiliates join us when we make runs?" I said puzzled. "And since when did we decide to make runs to L.A? Am I not the head leader of the Detroit sector? So why am I just now hearing about this shit?" I spat in pure anger.

"Keywords nigga, the Detroit sector! You ain't the leader of jack shit! I don't know who the fuck told you that you were the leader of this whole damn gang, but you got your shit highly fuckin' mistaken." J-ro began, causing my blood boil at the pure thought of me losing the control and power I had over this gang. How the fuck could I lose my control and power when I was on top of my shit?

"I'm not even the damn leader of this gang." J-ro announced, leaving me in shock. "What the fuck do you mean?" I asked in pure confusion. During the three years I've been in this fucking gang, I could have sworn that J-ro and X-block were the leaders of H-block. So what the fuck was this nigga saying?

I sat there as I watched him and all the other members laugh in my damn face. "What the fuck is so funny?" I yelled in anger. "Calm the fuck down nigga. I guess you didn't know huh?" J-ro replied. "Didn't know what?" I spewed. "The original and main two leaders of H-Block live in Cali." He began. "What the fuck?" I said in confusion.

"Yeah nigga, the two niggas are in Cali living their low-key life, making bread legally and illegally. They hired me and X-block as their front man, to make it look like we are the ones running the shit. When really they are the ones running the whole affiliation nationwide." He continued, with a proud smile planted on his face.

"So when do I get to meet these niggas?" I asked as I started to spark my blunt, already rolled up with the Kush. This was all too much for a nigga at one time. I had to spark a blunt to calm my nerves. "You will meet them next weekend when we head over to L.A. They asked to see you personally." J-ro explained. "Why?" I said, as I exhaled the smoke out of my mouth. "Don't trip nigga. They heard nothing but good things about you. Especially how you helped this gang come up on these streets of Detroit." Our fellow member X-Block chipped in. "Aiight then." I simply stated as I began to inhale the sweet Kush.

"So what about Cash and her affiliates?" I asked as I stared her down. "Why are you so worried about her nigga?" J-ro asked in automatic defense. "Why is yo' ass on defense nigga? Are you hittin' that or something nigga?" I snapped back as I stood up, ready to get buck with this punk bitch.

"Wouldn't you like to know nigga?" J-ro said as he stood up, like he really was going to do something. I was nowhere near scared of him. He wasn't even a real ass gangsta' in my eyes. He was just a regular worker off the street, who happened to get paid to be the leader's substitute. Shit at least Smooth and I wasn't scared to let niggas know that we ran our shit. We were real niggas, who did real things. After today, I couldn't take this shit seriously.

"Look, you don't want none. So if you're smart you would sit the fuck down." I said sternly, as I mugged him. "Or what?" He hollered. "You're acting real bad right now, like you about shit..." He began to talk shit, yet I wasn't hearing it. I was tired of hearing this little whack ass nigga talk shit. I swear he is two seconds away of getting merked, right here in this boardroom. "If it wasn't for me you wouldn't be shit! You ran to me, practically begging to be a part of this damn gang. You ain't shit and will never amount to shit." The voice of J-ro yelling at me quickly interrupted my thoughts.

"You ain't shit and will never amount to shit." The very last sentence lingered in my mind, tracing me back to my past when my father use to beat me with anything he could grab. I endured so much physical pain as he would constantly tell me that exact same thing J-ro slurred at me. I couldn't take anymore... I was tired of being flat out disrespected.

I grabbed my pistol from my boxers, and gripped it tightly as I aimed it at his head. Instead of seeing J-ro's shocked face expression, all I could see was flashbacks of my father's chocolate face in front of me. I pulled the trigger and blew J-ro's brains out, just like I did to my father when I was twelve years old. Today was my snapping point. I couldn't take this gang shit no more. I was tired of getting played like a fucking fool. I was beginning to self-destruct, and if I'm going down, then everyone else have to go down with me.

I showed the rest of the H-block niggas no mercy. Before they could even think about running out of the board room, I merked all of them. The only person left alive in this boardroom other than me, was Cashmere. I glared at her as she sat in her seat, shaking and screaming uncontrollably. "Shut the fuck up!" I commanded, as I walked over to her and pulled her out of her seat by her arm. I dragged her out the board room, and headed towards the front door.

"What are you doing Kris?" She cried. "You are coming with me. You are going to take me to see those little whack ass leaders of this bullshit, and you are going to help me put an end to this shit once and for all." I demanded, as I shoved her outside with my gun pressed against her back. She continued to sob heavily as we headed towards my back-up, all black marauder car. "Do we really have to do this Kris?" She pleaded. "Don't ask me fucking questions. Just do as I say." I started. "Now get your ass in the car. We are about to take a trip to L.A."

Simone

"Where the fuck have you been?" I yelled as I followed Jake into our bedroom. "Three days has passed and you just now show up at home? I know work doesn't keep you that fucking busy, to the point that you can't come home for three damn days? Shit you could have at least called nigga! Or were you too busy fuckin' that bitch to even pick up the damn phone and check in at home? Huh Jake? "I continued to go off.

"Simone don't start that shit with me tonight. I don't want to hear your mouth, so shut the fuck up!" Jake cursed, showing me a whole different perspective. The sweet and loving husband was gone. The tone of his voice was as if he was talking to a hoe out on the street. Yet I'm not a hoe off the street, I'm his wife! With an instant, I flipped.

"What Shit Jake?" I yelled angrily. "Don't start shit with you Jake! Yo' ass has been missing for three damn days and I'm suppose to just sit here and not say shit? Well you got the wrong fuckin' bitch." I yelled as I got all up in his face. "Get out of my face Simone." He commanded, as if he was going to do some physical harm to me. I laughed at the new balls this man grew. "Get out your face or what? What the fuck are you going to do to me if I don't? You're not about shit Jake! Let's face it, you're a weak ass bitch." I spat foully.

Before I could finish talking shit, Jake grabbed me by my neck, and violently slammed me against the wall. Shock and pain shot through my body, as I stared into his now burnt sienna colored eyes.

I couldn't believe that he would do such a violent act to me, yet as I looked into his eyes, I could not spot his soul. Looking into his eyes was like looking into the eyes of my enemies before I killed them, full of pure hate. "Don't fucking test me Simone! I'm not the man who will sit and let you have your way with. Fuck me over and that's your ass woman. Don't fuckin' test me or I will fuck you up." He spewed, as he tightened his grip around my neck. "You got that?" He commanded, placing a sense of fear into my body. "Yes." I murmured in pure fear. Jake released his grip from my neck, causing me to drop down to the ground.

Tears cascaded down my cheek as I watched him leave the room. I just don't understand how I could let this man bring me down to this level. After all I've been through with him, as his wife and as the mother of his child, I can't believe he would turn around and treat me like this!

My tears could not stop falling as I walked into our master bathroom, stood in front of the mirror, and I stared at myself. My make-up was smeared by my tears, heavy bags laid under my eyes, and my hair was rambled...I couldn't even recognize myself.

If a Negro did this to me back when I was "Krazy," I would have killed him on the spot! Yet here I 'am, being weak, crying, bitchass Simone. What has happened to me? I had to clear my mind of this confusion. I need to get out of here... I need to go for a drive. With that in mind, I quickly washed my face, and pulled myself together before I hopped into my car and drove off.

"Gurl, I don't know what is going on! Jayden won't even look at me, let alone touch me." Sweetz explained, expressing her issues of problematic marriage. Funny thing is, her problems are the same as mine, yet only minor compared to the incident I experienced today. I called Sweetz over for a girl talk at our favorite spot, which was the coffee shop. I couldn't clear my mind alone. I needed Sweetz to talk to me. Sweetz was like my sanity, keeping me sane in this crazy world we lived in.

"And he is being so mean to Mi'quel...I understand you taking your shit out on me, but don't take it out on our son. It's like he did a 180, I just don't understand." She sighed. "I don't either. Today was my breaking point with Jake...That fool done went crazy." I said, as I took a sip of my warm coffee. "What?" Sweetz exclaimed. I sighed before I explained my incident with Jake to her, I knew I wouldn't hear the end of this.

"Oh Hell the fuck no! Simone what the fuck? And you let that nigga get away with it?" Sweetz yelled, with astonishment written all over her face. "I can't believe this shit! Are you serious right now? I swear I'm about to kill a man!" She ranted, causing me to laugh. "Sweetz calm down." "Calm down?" She responded, as she looked at me like I was delusional.

"Simone I think you're the one being too calm about this shit. The old Krazy needs to come out and show his ass that you are not the one to be fucked with." Sweetz continued. I looked down at my cell phone, feeling guilty as charge. Sweetz was right, and I couldn't even deny it. "You're right...But Sweetz..." My voice trailed off, as I fought back the tears. "It's hard, when it's the one you love. I gave him my trust, my love, my everything ... We share a child for Christ sake!" I explained. "When he did that, I just didn't understand. Like why he would do this to me? Me? The woman who he loved so much...His wife, and the mother of his only child." I continued, as tears began to flow down my cheek.

"Aww sweetie." Sweetz said, as she grabbed my hand. "I understand your point, but if there is something that I learned from our past life...The most important lesson Smooth taught me was to never trust anyone. Even the one you love." She explained.

I watched as her mouth continued to move as she explained more, but I was still stuck on that sentence. *"To never trust the one you love."* How can you live a life not trusting the person, who you love and at one point gave all your trust to? That doesn't make sense at all! I couldn't receive that message, and I will not. That is the most ridiculous piece of advice I ever heard. Jake and I may not be perfect but I know that I can trust him. Right?

The loud ring of my cell phone interrupted both my thoughts, and the speech Sweetz was giving me. "Hold that thought." I said quickly, as I looked down at my cellphone screen, only to see a private number. No one has ever called my phone private since I been to L.A, but I was curious to know who it was.

"Hello." I answered. "Hello Krazy...Or is it Simone now?" The deep familiar voice trailed through my phone, causing my heart to sink. "Kris?" I said, puzzled at the thought. "You know it. The one and only baby." I could hear his smile through the phone, that dazzling smile that I once loved. But wait, "How did you get my number?" I interrogated. "Don't worry love, I got my ways. I heard you're out here in L.A playing house wife huh?" He said, quickly changing the subject. "Yeah, something you wish I would do for you." I jabbed in. "Hmm...I don't know about that love, we would be too busy handling business and running shit together. No time to have you sit at home and play housewife. I need a partner, not a bitch." Kris replied in his hardcore tone.

"Which is why we aren't together." I spat. "I see you're still a feisty one." He laughed. "I miss that trait. That was one thing I loved about you baby, you always was a hot head like me." He continued. "What do you want Kris?" I asked in annoyance.

"I want us to meet up and have a talk about some things." He answered. "Some things about what?" I scoffed. He laughed. "Aww Krazy, you were always the one to question me. Never the one to just agree and do it, you always have to know why, when, and how. But if you like your little happy go-lucky family, with your little whack ass husband, and your little son...Then I suggest you just listen to me. No questions asked."

"Fine...Where do you want to meet me at, cause I'm in L.A and there is no way in hell I'm flying back to Detroit." I replied. "Oh I'm in L.A too sweet thang." He joked. "Let's meet at the Suede Bar and Lounge at around seven. Nice little laid back spot, good place to you know...Chat." He suggested. "Fine I will see you then." "Yup." He said before hanging up on me. I sat in my chair in pure amazement, only to look up and see Sweetz giving me raised eyebrows. Oh gosh, here we go!

"What the fuck was that all about? Why was Kris calling your damn phone?" Sweetz interrogated me, like she was my woman or something. I couldn't help but laugh. "I don't know, but I'm going to find out." I simply replied. "Hmm, you better be careful fuckin' around with that nigga. You know Kris is nothin' but trouble." She said, as she folded her arms. "Yeah, but I got this. If not I will call you for backup." I joked. "Bitch you better call me. Or I'mma' kick both of ya'll asses!" She snapped.

"Oh shit! I gotta' go pick up little Mike from the pre-school, let me get my black ass on." Sweetz continued, while getting up and grabbing her leather jacket and huge Alexander McQueen bag. "Yeah let me go home and get ready for this little meeting tonight." I chimed in, as I grabbed my belongings, and headed towards the exit with her.

"You better call me as soon as you guys get done talking missy!" Sweetz demanded, as we headed into the parking lot. "Yes momma." I laughed. "I'm serious!" She exclaimed. "Ok. I will call you, now go and pick up your child woman!"

"Fine...I'm goin', I'm goin'...But you better call me hoe! Or I'm beating that ass..." She yelled out of her car window before heading off. I sat in my car and shook my head. All I could do was I laugh at Sweetz. I swear, what am I going to do without that crazy chick? Can't live with her, and for damn sure can't live without her! Now that I'm in a good disposition, it was time to go home, and get ready to meet up with the infamous Kris.

I made my way to the Suede lounge, anxious to see this old man of my past. I decided to show him what he's been missing, so I slipped into my very sleek and sexy black, Vera Wang dress that hugged my southern curves, and showed my double D's off nicely. My black Christian Louboutin gladiator heels brought an extra appeal to this outfit, as my long black hair was curled down to my mid-back.

I spotted Kris sitting in the back of the club, dressed in a black button up with a red tie, some black slacks, and some black and red chucks. I was surprised to see that he switched from his Detroit hood style to the causal L.A attire. His now long hair was pulled back into a low ponytail, as his beard was nicely trimmed. I must say, he was looking very scrumptious. I switched slowly over to his table, while he eyed me like an eagle eying its prey.

"Well hello Kris." I smiled, as I sat in front of him. "Hello Krazy, long time no see." He replied with his grin, that I once thought was sexy. "Yes it has been a long time." I said as I sipped on my Chardonnay. "You look good, I must say. You've gotten all thick and sexy... Sexier than last time I seen you. Damn girl!" Kris complimented, as he gazed at me and bit his bottom lip. That one move use to lure me back into his bedroom, but not tonight!

"You look nice too." I simply replied. "Remember when we use to get it in at the clubs? Up in V.I.P, not caring if anyone was watching us." Kris said, reminiscing over our past. "Ugh, let's not talk about our past Kris, you said you wanted to talk about something serious so let's get down to business shall we?" I said, getting to the point. "Straight? It's like that huh?" "Yeah it's like that these days...I'm not one to sit and waste time over bullshit, you know that Kris." I answered harshly. "Hmmm...Yeah I guess it's like that when my ex-partner and lover is playing housewife to a little whack ass wanna-be." Kris snapped, as he took a sip of his scotch.

"What are you talking about Kris?" I said puzzled. "My husband is not some wanna-be. He is a successful realtor and the father of my child. He is a good man." I explained, as Kris began laughing. "Are you sure about that? Do you really know the man you are dealing with? Or are you married to a total stranger, who could be your own worst enemy?" Kris asked, quickly reverting to his serious manner. All I could say to this was "What?"

"Do you really think you can leave the Hot Boyz and start a new life, without the gang life haunting you?" Kris said, as he stared at me with his gray eyes. "What are you talking about Kris?" I said, cutting him off in confusion. "Niggas ain't loyal no more Krazy! The streets ain't the same as they were when the Hot Boyz was out. These new gangs are scandalous and they play by a new game. I'm not saying that the game we played was fair back then, but the shit that's going on right now is just fucked up." Kris continued.

"Kris, you can't even talk about loyalty. Your ass turned against everyone! Smooth, the Hot Boyz...Shit even me!" I exclaimed. "I know Krazy, but you don't understand why I did that...You never will." Kris sighed, as he looked down at his glass.

"No one is who you think they are Krazy. Smooth was my closest friend, my right hand man...But where the fuck is he now? Huh?" He ranted. "Exactly, no fuckin' where. He left his baby momma high 'n' dry and let the damn gang fall apart at the worst time. What kind of niggas does that?" He continued. "Tell me Krazy, what kind of nigga does that?" Kris shouted, causing a scene in the lounge. "Calm the fuck down. This is not the time, nor place to create a scene." I said whispered. "Aiight, then answer me damnit!" Kris commanded, as I shook my head at his crazy antics.

"Kris...Did you ever think that he might've got killed? While you're over there talkin' shit, he could be dead for all we know." I suggested. "Dead?" Kris laughed. "That nigga ain't dead! Low-key, he's closer to us then we think he is..." Kris leaned in. "There are eyes everywhere baby. I don't care what state you move to, there are eyes everywhere." He whispered. I looked at him like he was crazy. This man is fuckin' insane!

"Kris what the fuck are you talking about?" I spat. "Krazy listen to me..." He grabbed my hand. "I'm not just talking for my health here. This shit is real, you can't trust anyone. Not even that little nigga you think you love. He's not the man you think he is. Him and his brother." Kris said, causing me to get irritated at his insanity. "His brother? Really Kris, you had to add his brother in this shit. A man of God, are you foreal?" I questioned him in disgust. "And what the fuck does that mean? Shady is shady, no matter how much you try to cover it up. These niggas ain't good

Simone." Kris explained. I knew Kris was serious when he called me by my real name.

"If they aren't good, then what are they Kris? Who are they?" I snapped back. Kris looked around the room, making sure no one was watching us, before he leaned in closer and began to speak.

"Jake and Jayden are our worst enemies...They are the original leaders of the H-block. They've been in this gang shit way too deep. They hired these niggas named J-ro and X-block to be their front man to act like they are the leaders. Yet they are over here making the major moves." As he continued to go on and on, I went deaf. I couldn't even hear any more of his bullshit. I couldn't believe the shit he was saying. Is he really trying to tell me that Jake and Jayden are the notorious gang leaders of our rival gang? They can't be the leaders of H-block...They just can't.

"This shit is real Simone. That nigga Jayden killed Killa' Mike. And Jake...That nigga is just scandalous as hell. They've been trying to get their revenge against me and Smooth for as long as I can remember, especially since we killed off their affiliates in Detroit. I've been out here on these streets, doing my research on these niggas." He said, leaving me in amazement.

"So if they are who you say they are, what the fuck are they doing with me and Sweetz?" I said as I folded my arms, and stared at him with a raised eyebrow. "Simone, have you been fuckin brainwashed yo'?" Kris shook his head. "I know you are smarter than that...C'mon baby, use your head! Why would some niggas who is against us, be messing with you, the girlfriends of the leaders from their rival gang?" Kris hinted. I just stared at him in disbelief. "You of all people should know this, if they can't get close to us, the next best thing is their girls and family. That's our biggest liability and their greatest revenge." Kris explained as he took another sip of his scotch.

"These niggas knew about you and Sweetz before you even thought about moving to L.A. You guys made it so easy for them because you fell into their plot. They knew your exact location, made their way into your life, and established a close relationship with you. Shit, they even married you and played family man and shit, and this whole time, they just been waiting." He paused.

"Waiting for what?" I asked impatiently. "Waiting to kill you." He answered, leaving me in shock. "What? What? What?" I asked repeatedly. "That's been their whole plan baby...This whole time. These men are assigned as hit men, plotting to kill you and your kids. Especially since I took out the H-block niggas in Detroit! I'm sorry to say, but the time is approaching soon. You probably noticed a sudden change in these niggas. They ain't all lovey-dovey no more huh?" He chuckled. As much as I didn't want to admit it, he was right, Jake and Jayden has made a sudden change.

"And you don't understand why huh? Cause baby it's time for war. I killed their men off, so now they have to kill what will hurt me deeper than anything else in this world...And that's you baby." He said sincere. I could see the truth in his eyes, but I just couldn't receive all of what he told me.

"That's why I'm here Krazy. I can't just sit and let this shit happen. I had to tell you, and you have to tell Sweetz ASAP! We have to be ten steps ahead of these niggas, we have to come together and get the burner out on these niggas." "But...I love him, I have a son with him...I-I can't." I struggled to finish my sentence. "You don't love him Krazy...He's not the man you think he is...He is our enemy. It's a dog-eat-dog world baby. It's either them or us. Keep that in mind baby. I'm planning on taking this nigga out tomorrow night, but I would need more man power. I need you and Sweetz to help me bring these niggas down." Kris replied.

"Tomorrow night?" I repeated. "Yes...We don't have fuckin' time to waste Krazy. We know too much, and they know that...So they are ready to take us out. We can't let them win baby, we have to get rid of these niggas and end this gang shit for good." He took a sip of his drink.

"I'm tired of living this gang life Simone. I never really had a life you know? Since we were eight, we been out on these streets hustling, grinding, gang-banging...I just want a clean slate. I want you back baby, I love you. Let's just do this last move and get it right." He said, as he looked at me with those sad eyes and held my hand. I looked at him almost giving in, until I thought about our incident at Mike's funeral. Hell no, Kris is shady as fuck now, I can't trust him. This nigga could be just trying to ruin the life I set up for myself, just to feed into his little power kick. Fuck that!

I quickly snatched my hand away from him as I stood up, and looked at him in disgust. "Fuck you Kris!" I started. "I can't believe you would pull this shit out of ya' ass! Just so you can ruin my life. You think I'm going to sit here and believe you after all the shit you put me through? Hell no. Fuck you!" I yelled. Kris leaned back in his seat and looked at me, before he spoke calmly.

"Ok Krazy, if that's how you want it to be, then fine! But you can't say I didn't warn you. My days on this earth are numbered, but I couldn't leave without at least trying to save you baby. But hey, if you want to think and believe this shit he brainwashed yo' ass with, then fine, that's your life. All I'm saying is, keep your eyes and ears open, and tomorrow night you know where I will be. So if you change your mind, come and find me."

I looked at him in disgust for the last time before I made my way to the exit. I couldn't believe the shit he said to me, I wanted nothing else to do with him and his schemes, good riddance!

As I sat in my car parked in front of my house, I immediately called Sweetz and told her everything that happened between Kris and I. "Damn, I don't even know what to believe. Kris wouldn't just say shit for no reason Simone." She said through the phone.

"Man Kris is the lowest scum in the game, how can we believe that nigga?" I retorted. "I don't know Simone, let's just be on our toes with this one. Let's keep our eyes and ears open like he said, because we never know who to trust with shit like this." Sweetz explained, yet I wasn't hearing it. "Yeah, okay. Well I'm at my house, so I will call you later ok?" I said, trying to end this conversation. "Ok girl, be safe." She said. "Yeah I will, bye girl." I said before I hung up. This was all too much in one night, all I wanted to do was just lay down with my son, and call it a night.

I quietly entered the dark house and made my way upstairs. I knew Jake was here because I saw the light coming from his office, and heard his whispers echoing throughout the silent house. Even the quietest whispers in this house can become an echo, which can be a good and bad thing.

"Keep your eyes and ears open." The voice of Kris replayed in my head, as I stood against the wall of the hallway near his office. I needed to find out for myself, just what kind of man I was dealing with, so I began to listen. "This shit has been going on for too long. I even got married and had a kid with this broad. This was not a part of the fuckin' plan! I'm tired of this shit. That bitch ass nigga Kris killed off our men, its fuckin' war Jayden! Yeah, so when are we going to kill these bitches?" I covered my mouth, trying my best not to just scream out of shock. I couldn't believe what I was hearing. This shit was real, and Kris was not just pulling shit out of his ass. This shit was real!

"Yeah nigga today is Monday...Yo' ass is getting old." He laughed. "Yeah...Tomorrow isn't a good day for killing. How about Wednesday? That's good huh? Yeah. Wednesday we will take them and them little dumbass kids out. Shit I know you are tired of playing daddy to that little bastard, looking like that Mike nigga you merked." He continued, leaving me in pure disgust.

I couldn't take hearing this anymore. I had to get the fuck out of this house, but I can't make it obvious. I have to be cautious because if I slip up just one time, he will know that I'm up on his scheme. I had to be ten steps ahead of him, and in order to do that, I had to play along with his game. Simone was no longer here anymore, Krazy is finally back. It was time to make some silent moves. With that in mind, I crept into our bedroom, sent Sweetz a text message telling her everything, and began thinking of a plan. I was in so much denial thinking that I had a perfect man and a perfect life. Yet all this shit was a fuckin' trap! I was living, eating, and sleeping with my hit man! A man who was waiting to kill me and my child...I guess Kris was right after all!

<u>Kris</u>

I sat in my black Nissan, parked across the alley on Melrose St. DMX "How It's Going Down" played softly as I sparked up my blunt full of Kush to help calm my nerves. The words of this song were so real in relation to my life with Krazy. It was nice to see baby girl one more time before shit pops off. She gotten so thick and beautiful, too bad she is stuck on stupid with that weak ass, fake of a man. I knew we ended off on rocky terms, but I still had mad love for her.

Unfortunately, I knew that things were going to change after I kill her little husband tonight. I had Cashmere arrange a little set up with Jake and Jayden tonight. She would lead him over to this alley and I would come and get rid of these little niggas. Ending this gang shit once and for all.

"The time has come," was what Cashmere texted me, letting me know that she had them at the spot. Perfect timing; since I just finished this blunt, and I was ready to merk 'em. I made my way over to the dark alley, where I could see the silhouette of Cashmere and two others. Their backs were facing me as they chatted with Cashmere, not even sensing my presence. I approached them, ready to see Jake and Jayden face to face.

"Well hello mothafuckas'!" I gloated, as I gripped my guns placed in both hands. The two turned around and finally revealed themselves to me. But wait, that's not Jake and Jayden!

Instead, I was standing in front of the infamous siblings, Liyah and Smooth. Liyah's long black hair was corn rowed down to her mid back. Her silver eyebrow piercing gleamed under the streetlight, as her cold black eyes pierced through my soul. Never have I seen Liyah like this; she was dressed in a black hoodie, black baggy jeans that I could wear myself, and some black and white Jordan 23's. If I didn't know her previously, I would have thought she was a damn man...One of those pretty niggas that could pass for either a male or a rough ass female.

"Well, well, well...We meet again." Smooth said, with a devious smile. His smile was the only thing that made me recognize him. His long braids were now cut off as he sported 360 waves, and his honey colored eyes was now covered with dark brown contacts. He looked like a different person!

Dressed in a black leather top coat, his black baggy jeans folded over his black timbs, and his hands were covered by some black leather gloves. I knew something was up. The only time Smooth wore leather gloves was when he was ready to pull a trigger on somebody. I'm guessing that somebody would be me.

As I stood there contemplating my next move, Cashmere walked over to Liyah grinning like a Cheshire cat. Liyah wrapped her arm around Cashmere's waist, kissing her gently on the lips, before they turned and looked at me. They were lovers! What type of sick and twisted shit is this? I couldn't even believe what I was seeing, this shit is just all fucked up.

"Cashmere, what the fuck is this?" I asked. "This is what you wanted, an arrangement right?" She smiled. "Don't play fuckin' games with me bitch...You set me up!" I yelled. "No sweetheart, you set your own self up." She replied calmly.

"You knew your time was up. Don't act like you didn't know. You can't go around betraying niggas in a gang and think that this shit isn't going to catch up with you." She continued. "You got the game fucked up homeboy." Smooth pitched in.

"What the fuck are you doing here?" I asked, as I gripped my gun tightly. "I'm here to handle some business." Smooth answered. "And what the fuck does this shit have to do with me?" I spat. "Everything..." He said, as he sparked up a Cuban cigar. "Heard that you were trying to take out my brothers." Smooth continued. "Your brothers?" I asked confused. "The only brother you had was Mike and that mothafucka' is dead. Shit, the only people I'm tryin' to take out is..." I stopped in the middle of my sentence. What the fuck?

"Your brothers are Jake and Jayden, the leaders of H-block!" I froze in shock. Before I could make a move, I felt the barrel of a gun pressed against the back of my head.

"Good to see that you could join us Jake?" Smooth smiled. "Jake?" I questioned. "Surprise, surprise huh?" Jake chuckled from behind me. "My other brother Jayden couldn't make it...But one brother is good enough." Smooth said. "These niggas can't be your brothers." I commented, still cautious of the gun that was pressed behind my head.

"Didn't think that my dad Big Man got around huh?" He continued. "Your dad?" "Yes my dad! The man you fuckin' killed that night over Krazy. Guess you didn't know that I was sitting in the car that night huh?" Smooth explained. I could not only hear the hatred in his voice, but I could feel it. "Ten years old, having to drive myself back to the house, because my father got his head blown off." He said, as he stared at me in disgust.

"So this whole fuckin' time you knew huh? Since you know so fuckin' much, guess you knew how fuckin' guilty I felt for killin' my own fuckin' uncle! Guess you knew how many nights I had nightmares, how I seen him hovering over me in the dark when I was tryin' to sleep huh? I guess you know just how fucked up I' am in the head? Huh do you?" I yelled full of anger. "I killed not only my uncle, but I killed my own father. So since you know so fuckin' much then you would know how fucked up I' am mentally. All you're doing is adding fuel to my fuckin' fire!"

"Do you think I really give two fucks?" Smooth chuckled. "Because of you , my whole fuckin' life changed. My mom committed suicide. She couldn't deal with the fact that her husband wasn't just a business man like he told her. Instead he was a notorious drug lord, who had two other sets of families, one in Cali and one in New York. She couldn't handle that deceit and betrayal of the man she loved so much, and I ended up watching my own fuckin' mother shoot herself right in front of my eyes." Smooth started to explain, reminiscing over his fucked up childhood.

"There was no one to take care of us, I had to be the care taker of the family and take over the streets like my father. I brought my brother and sister up to Detroit, got them involved, and I ended up losing my baby brother to this shit. All because of you!" He spat.

"Because of me? Nigga your brother raped his own fuckin' cousin and didn't even know it. You lost your little brother through the hands of your own fuckin' half-brother from Cali, and your trying to blame shit on me. How sick and fucked up is that?" I exclaimed.

"Mike wasn't playing by the rules. You live by the rules, you die by the rules. You know the game. Mike fucked up, so in the end he got put out the game." Smooth said coldly, as if he didn't give two fucks about his brother. I couldn't believe how cold he had become. I guess you never know a person until shit goes down, and now I'm seeing his true colors. Smooth is as vindictive and conniving as they come. He knew all about this shit from the beginning, and waited until now to get his revenge. Out of all the people in the Hot Boyz clique, I thought Smooth was the sane one of out the group, but now I see that he's just as fucked up as I' am. It's sad how the game can change us.

"But that's not all you did...Not only did you kill my father, but you fucked my girl multiple times." He stated, quickly interrupting my thoughts. Flashbacks of me sexing Sweetz during those late nights at the Hot Boyz mansion, while everyone was asleep, cruised through my mind. I couldn't help but to smile at the thought. "Yeah, I fucked that sweet little pussy..." I started, but was cut off by Smooth's fist connecting to my jaw. That hit caught me off guard, causing me to fall back onto the ground. Jake, Cashmere, and Liyah stood there and watched as Smooth hopped on top of me, and finished what he started.

"You fuckin' bitchmade nigga!" He yelled, as he continued to punch the shit out of me. "Yo', yo' back up off of him." Liyah yelled out, as she pulled Smooth off of me. "There's no need to fight this nigga. He's goin' to get taken care of soon enough."

Taken care of...What the fuck? I quickly got up off the ground, grabbed my gun, and fired shots at Liyah, Smooth, and Cashmere as I ran off. I knew I hit Liyah because I heard her scream out in pain, but that didn't stop me from running. I was almost out of this alley. I could see my car parked at the end of the street. All I had to do was hop in my car, and get the hell out of dodge. I was almost there, ducking and dodging the bullets that Smooth and Jake shot at me.

Right before I reached the corner, a large group of niggas approached me, blocking my exit. All of them holding their burners, ready to merk me. I looked down at all of their guns, directed towards me, and I instantly knew there was no way out of this one. I was trapped. I glared at them, as they glared at me, ready to get this shit over with. I'm staring face to face with my death, caused by my past lies, deceit, and betrayal. My time has come.

<u>Sweetz</u>

"Are you ready Sweetz?" Simone asked, as we sat in my rental car. Today was the day. It was seven o'clock on a Wednesday morning, and the plan was in full effect. "You take the kids with you, and you don't call me until I call you. Just go straight to the spot ok?" She continued. "Okay. You be safe." I replied. "I will." She ensured, as she stepped out of my car. She looked into the backseat and stared at her son sitting in his car seat, sleeping peacefully.

"I can't believe that our lives fell down to this." She sighed. "Yeah, but shit we gotta' do what we gotta' do." I said, as I stared at her tear stained face.

"Always...I will call you when all of this shit is done. Just be safe and take care of my baby." She replied, before she walked away, leaving me responsible for not just my son, but for hers. There was nothing else to say, it was time to make moves. I started up my car, and began to head onto the highway...fleeing to another state.

Simone

I watched as Sweetz drove off with my son in her car. I had no more time to cry, and definitely no time to be scared. It was time to make moves. Time to get rid of the ones who betrayed us, and were waiting to get rid of us. My first victim was Jayden.

Sweetz sedated him before she left, leaving him as an easy target. I crept into his house and made my way upstairs to his bedroom. I stood there, staring at him in pure disgust, as he laid in his bed. The nerve of this man, to deceive my friend for this fucking long, and think he was going to get away with it. Hmm, he's has another thing coming!

I grabbed the bottle of whiskey off his counter, and began to pour it over his body. Unlike the time I killed Quick from the AK47 boyz, I came prepared this time with a small pack of matches. I struck a match, threw it on his body, and made my way downstairs. I didn't have time to waste. I had to make this look like a regular fire before the neighborhood wakes up. I rushed into the kitchen, cut the stove on, and threw the kitchen towel over the fire...Letting nature take its course. I quickly made my exit out the back door, like nothing happened. I had one down, and one more to go.

I sat in my car, staring at the picture of Jake and I on our wedding day, so many thoughts began to run through my mind. Who would have thought that this is where I would end up? After finally having what was mine, what I deserved, shit... What I fucking earned. This is it? All the blood, the sweat, and the tears that was shed for me to end up here! Who would've thought? As I sat parked across the street from his house, I stared off into space, thinking about what I was about to do. I took a deep breath before pulling out my glock, and quietly yet quickly got out of my car.

I took cautious steps as I headed towards the back of the house. With the security code imprinted in my memory, I cut off our alarm system. Sliding the glass door open, I snuck into the house and crept up the spiral staircase. I quietly entered our room where I spotted him lying there, sleeping so peacefully.

Tears started to form in my eyes as I cocked the gun, and aimed it at his head. This was not any, random guy. This was my Husband, my love, my heart, and the father of my child! Just then he stirred in his sleep, and his eyes slowly began to open. The tears started to cascade down my face as I pulled the trigger............ BOOM!

"What the fuck!" Jake jumped up after my bullet just barely brushed past his head, and hit the headboard. "What the fuck are you doing Simone?" Jake asked, as he stood in front of me, covering up his manhood with a pillow. My gun was still pointed at him, as he stood there in the nude, shaking, looking like a little bitch.

"Baby, why are you doing this?" He pleaded. "Don't fuckin' baby me! I know what yo' ass was up to this whole time nigga." I said angrily. "Do you really? What do you know Simone? Tell me what my ass was up to!" He yelled. "I know that you and Jayden were the leaders of H-block this whole fuckin' time, and that you were plotting to kill me, Sweetz, and the kids." I revealed.

"The fuckin' kids though Jake? If that's even your real fuckin' name...Or is it Black?" I continued. Jake laughed instantly. "What the fuck are you laughing at?" I said, as my blood boiled. "You think you know all about this shit, but really you have no clue." He said with a smirk. "What the fuck else is there to know, other than you wanting to kill me and our son?" I said in pure disgust. "Shit is deeper than what you think...None of these niggas is on your side! None!" He started.

"What, you thought them damn Hot Boyz was your fuckin friends? You thought them niggas had yo' back? They ain't shit...They are just as worst as me and I'm your fuckin hit man!" He ranted. "Shit to be honest with you, you can consider me doing you a fuckin' favor for trying to kill you and lil' Jake off, cause either way you're going to die in this game...It's just a matter of time." He said foul as hell.

Jake

My hands started to shake as I ranted on and on, telling this dumb bitch what was really was goin' on. Out of nowhere this bitch started to laugh hysterically. "Bitch what the fuck you laughing at? You think this shit a game?" I snapped, as I surveyed her face. She had this crazed face expression, a face I have never seen before. "You done talking that bullshit?" She said, still laughing. "How 'bout this, you lay back down in the bed, close those pretty eyes of yours, and this will be over before you know it." Simone explained with a seductive smile. "Bitch is you out your mind? Did you hear anything I told yo ass?" I flipped. She sighed heavily before tapping her foot against the floor, and rubbing the gun against her temple.

"Jakey...Jakey...My sweet husband of mine, I heard everything that came out yo' mouth...But obviously you ain't hear me well enough, I want yo' black ass to lay in the bed, so I can handle what I need to handle, and then I can leave...Now you can make this hard or easy, that's yo' choice...But listen, and you listen good...I ain't leaving this house 'til you are laying lifeless in your own pool of blood. You got that homie?"

This bitch must really be out of her fucking mind talking to me like this. This bitch just doesn't know who I 'am in these streets. Nigga I run mothafucking L.A! "Man you talking good, but what are you going to do about it?" As soon as those words left my mouth, a loud bang went off, and a stinging pain shot up in my mid-thigh. I looked down and saw a little graze wound that was so close to my dick...I lost it!

"Bitch what the hell!" I yelled, as she smiled that sexy smile of hers. "Next time I won't miss! Now lay on the fucking bed!" At that moment, I rushed her and started to struggle for the gun. To my surprise she was strong as hell. She head butted me in the nose, causing me to fall back. I stumbled trying to catch my balance, but was caught off guard when she busted my head with the gun. Warm liquid was leaking everywhere.

I held the side of my head, while I staggered to the side of the bed, reaching for my gun. Before I could grab it, she rushed me, and pushed me onto the bed. With one knee in my nuts, she quickly grabbed the pillow and smothered my face. Everything went black. My air started to get thin...Fuck, I can't die like this. Where did I go wrong with this? Now I remember, I fell in love with her. I underestimated her from the very beginning. I guess in the end she was the one I couldn't trust....

Sweetz

"Damnit!" I cursed under my breath, as I realized that my gas tank was now prevailing to empty. "Ooo..." Mi'quel giggled from the backseat. "Mommy you cussed!" He gleamed. "Mommy you cussed...Ooo you cussed!" He began to sing, yet getting on my last damn nerve. "Hush baby." I said, as I pulled off to the closest exit.

Many cars were behind me, yet I couldn't help but notice this black 2010 Audi, that has been behind me this whole time. Then again, maybe I'm just being paranoid. I quickly ran into the gas station, leaving Mi'quel and Jake in the car. I figured that it wouldn't take long to pay for some damn gas, so the kids should be ok.

"Hello sexy." the Arabic man behind the counter smiled. "Umm, hello. I would like to put fifty on pump six please." I said, blowing off his compliment. "Can I get your number with that too?" He asked, as he took my money. "No, can you hurry up please." I rushed impatiently. "Geesh, in a hurry huh?" He said as he stared at me, with my damn money still in his hand.

"It would be nice if you did your damn job, and take my money so I can go pump some damn gas into my car. I have two little ones that I left in the car, and I don't have time for your games!" I went off. "Two little ones?" He said puzzled, as he looked out the window in the direction of my car. "Ma'am there is no one in your car. I don't even see any car seats. So what little ones are you talking about?" He continued as he looked at me like I was crazy. Without another word spoken, I ran out the gas station towards my car, only to see my car empty. No kids. No car seats. My heart sunk deeply, as I began to panic.

"Mi'quel!" I screamed loudly, as I looked around the gas station parking lot. "Jake? Mi'quel? "I continued to scream out, as everyone looked at me like I was delusional. "Somebody kidnapped my kids' damnit! Call 911." I cried uncontrollably.   As I looked around the parking lot, I noticed that the black Audi that was following me was no longer parked. I knew without a doubt, that whoever was in that car kidnapped the kids.

My cell phone rung loudly, breaking my thoughts. Without even looking at the screen, I answered. "Hello." "Missing something?" The deep voice replied from the other end. "Where the fuck are my kids?" I yelled into the phone. "Oh no Sweetz, yelling at me won't make it any better. Don't worry about the little ones. They are safe with me. Especially my son." He continued, causing my heart to sink even lower. "Smooth?" I said in shock. How could this be?

"The one and only baby. Did you really think that I was going to just up and leave my son like that? C'mon now baby, you know me better than that." He chuckled. "Well maybe you don't, but you're surely going to find out." He started, but was cut off by me yelling into the phone.

"Don't you dare touch those kids Smooth! You hurt them and I will fuckin' hunt you down and skin your ass alive!" "Is that a threat mami?" He asked. "No nigga, that's a fuckin' promise." I replied coldheartedly.

"I hope you can back it up mami, it would be such a shame to have to kill you along with these little kids." Smooth replied. "You wouldn't do that shit Smooth!" "You don't know what the fuck I would do...Keep testing me bitch." He threatened. "Now if you want to see these little niggas again, then you need to do exactly what the fuck I tell you from now on. You got it?" He commanded. "Yeah, I got it." I sighed. "Now get in the car and get back on the highway until I tell you what to do next." With that said, I hopped in the car and followed his commands, all in the pursuit to get the kids back.

<u>Simone</u>

It was all over with. The deed was done. No more lies, no more betrayal, no more Hot Boyz, no more gangs, and no more of this fucked up lifestyle for me. When I killed Jake, I killed it all. As I sped down the highway, I felt a new freedom. Things were about to change. I grabbed my phone and dialed Sweetz's number.

"It's all done girl. It's all done!" I gloated. "No!" She shrieked. "They're fuckin' onto us Simone! They're on to us!" She yelled frantically. "What the fuck do you mean that they're onto us?" I asked confused. "They're on to us!" She repeated loudly this time, like that's supposed to help me know who she is talking about.

"Jake and Jayden is dead, so who the fuck is on to us?" I asked. "They took the fuckin' kids. They took our fuckin kids!" She cried, causing my heart to sink. "Sweetz who the fuck took our kids? How the fuck could they have taken our kids?" I yelled angrily. "They're on to us Simone..." She sobbed like a baby.

I couldn't take this shit. She wasn't telling me shit that I needed to hear. I placed the phone on speakerphone and dropped it in the passenger seat. "If you don't tell me who the fuck..." I started to go off, but was cut off by the loud sound of police sirens behind me.

I looked up through my rearview mirror, only to see a flock of police cars speeding behind me. I couldn't speed off and flee like I wanted to, because these damn black Audi's were in my way, driving slow as hell. Fuck! How could I have gotten caught? We had this shit planned out perfectly.

As soon as I pulled over, the two black Audi's sped off with a quickness. "They're on to us." The voice of Sweetz traveled through my mind, and suddenly it clicked. This was a fuckin' set-up! Everything this whole time was a fuckin' set-up!

Unraveling the secrets hidden in their

closets

T.L. Joy & Simone Majors takes it to another level, exposing those behind the set-up

in...

"Framed"

What do you do when everyone who was for you, is now against you? What do you do when the only person who had your back is now DEAD, leaving you in a deadly game of corruption and street power? Welcome to the world of Simone "Krazy" Simmons. After spending four years in prison due to a cruel set up, plotted by the ones she thought she loved, she's now back on the streets full of heat. Seeking revenge on the most powerful of all the street gangs, Krazy is on a chase to conquer what's rightfully hers.....Her four year old Son! Hell hath no fury than a woman scorned, especially when it's a Krazy Bitch!

Coming Soon!

CPSIA information can be obtained
at www.ICGtesting.com
Printed in the USA
LVOW10s1605090617
537561LV00011B/568/P